PRE

When George Orwell set (
in 1946, he began with the following advice.

'Never use a metaphor, simile or other figure of speech which you are used to seeing in print.'

In other words, avoid clichés - like the plague. This basic tenet of good writing is drummed into anyone who sets out to learn the craft. And looking at the Oxford Languages definition of 'cliché', it's clearly good advice. What writer would want to employ 'a phrase or opinion that is overused and betrays a lack of original thought'?

But there's another recommendation about creativity that flatly contradicts this notion. And that is, to be truly original you have to break some rules.

In this collection of short stories, five writers have actively embraced the colourful figures of speech in the English language and used them as springboards for the imagination.

Each story is inspired by a cliché, but that's where their similarity ends. The stories encompass a wide range of styles and topics, from comedy to tragedy. In telling their tales each writer has, in their own unique way, engaged with various forms of figurative speech: metaphor, personification, oxymoron, conceit, hyperbole, irony, simile, exaggeration... take your pick and enjoy.

Out of the Blue

Dawn Morgan

Red was the first to go. I watched it fade as I stood at the sink, my eyes on a bloom at the top of a rose bush. It seemed to blanch through pink and cream to a pale shade, not quite white. I shook my head like a dog in a stream, but the strange blank stared back at me, a gap in life. And then, so fast that it shook the air out of my lungs, it spread from the top down, until the whole shrub was clothed in pale blots.

I thought at first that the rose was sick, but the off-white wash soon seeped to all my red plants: shades of blood, port and fire were soon as bland as milk. Man-made reds were next: the back door, which had a new coat of gloss last week, went through the same swift change. My old coat, hung on a peg. A glazed pot by the fence. All were bleached, in the space of a breath.

The phone rang. It was my son, Ian.

'Did you see it?' he asked. 'What do you think it means?'

'I don't know,' I told him. 'It's so odd.' My hands shook. My voice did too.

'Shall I come round?' he asked.

'No, don't.' It would be a long drive for him. 'There's no need. I'm fine.'

'Well, call me if you change your mind.'

'I will, thanks.'

He hung up, but I kept the phone to my ear as I watched a dull patch begin to grow in the sky.

It took more than two weeks for blue to leave us. Red had gone in an hour, but it seemed as if each shade of blue spent a day or two in its death throes before it passed the pale germ to its next of kin. We watched in dull pain as we lost them: sky blue and teal; all the deep tones of the sea; the bruised shade of trees; the puff of a bird's chest; clouds filled with young rain fresh from the coast.

The death rate rose in a steep curve as the last blues stretched out, like ink in the sun. I heard that a mass jump had been staged at Worms Head. The first group to go, but not the last. They leaped hand in hand with their eyes closed from the top of the cliff, a blind pack with no hope. The trend grew and crowds lined up to fall like leaves into the sea.

For a while, those of us who stayed got used to our new world. We had the sun, and warm fields of corn, and green fields, and all our trees. But of course, we knew what was to come.

Some of us talked of a move to the Pole. If we could go north, we thought, to a world that was meant to be white, it would seem less strange when the last hues left the earth. But we soon changed our minds. The death rate in the far north was much worse than here at home.

'Ice is blue,' said Ian, his voice flat. 'When that goes, you're lost. You can't see a thing.'

I felt cold at the thought of that flat, dead world. Like the one we would all have to face, some day.

I first saw green start to fade in a scarf I wore. I had looped it round my neck and glanced down to tie a knot when a faint patch seemed to grow on its edge. This time there was no long, drawn out death. The change was as quick as fire. It licked at the cloth and scorched it bare. Then I watched it spread.

We were left in a dun, grey world and the queues to reach the cliffs grew long. As if that form of death were the sole means to leave the earth. The last rite of man: a leap of no faith. When my turn came, I gripped Ian's hand and gave him a smile. There were no words we could think of, and we both knew there was no need to speak, to say how we felt.

There was fear of course, but as I looked at him for the last time I was filled with joy: my son's eyes, which had been grey all his life, were now as clear as the pale, new sky and I could see through them, as far as his soul.

UGLY AS SIN *and other clichés*

Every Picture Tells a Story

Kathy Miles

If it was a painting, you'd say it was surreal.

We'd been forced to stop because the road ended abruptly beside a gas station, and now we stared out of the windows in disbelief. We could see three red gas pumps and an office. There were dense woods beyond it, thick rows of dark impenetrable trees. It looked as if we'd come to the end of the world. Carly and I got out of the car. There was a man standing by the gas pumps: the attendant, we guessed. The forecourt was flooded with light, bright fluorescents that lit up the fringes of grass around the dusty road.

'Now what?' Carly asked. We were on a trip round America, and were meant to be heading for Northampton in Massachusetts, to stay with her friend Amy. Carly had done the trip before and suggested a shortcut, so we'd turned off the highway some twenty miles back, the road becoming narrower as we went. I thought she knew where she was going, but we'd obviously taken a wrong turn.

'Well, I guess we ask the guy which way we go. We don't want to be stuck here all night.'

'Too right,' I shivered, pulling my coat tight across

my chest. 'It's already getting colder.'

The attendant hadn't moved since we drew up, hadn't even glanced at us. But there was light inside the gas station office as well as outside. Maybe there was someone else there.

'We should fill the car up anyway,' Carly said.

We went over to the man. He didn't move.

'Hello there,' Carly said, her voice sounding very English, very upper-class.

'He didn't hear you.'

It was then, with some surprise, we realized the man was not real. Someone had made a life-sized cardboard model of an attendant, and put it up against the pumps. It was horribly realistic. He was dressed in old-fashioned trousers, waistcoat and tie, and his hair was cut very short. We backed away. This was weird. Normal people didn't put models onto gas pumps in the middle of nowhere, did they? I mean, who the hell would see it? There were no houses around, nothing but the road and the forest. Come to that, why was there a gas station anyway, when the road didn't lead anywhere?

'Bloody hell,' said Carly, 'we should get out of here.'

Memories of horror films, watched in the safety of the student lounge, came back to us. *Psycho* was in my mind. I was pretty sure Carly was thinking the same thing.

'Maybe there'll be someone in that office? Someone real?'

Carly looked at me as if I'd gone mad.

'Ellen, we need to go. We need to go *now*. This place is freaking me out.'

I wandered over to the building. It was empty. Not a soul in sight. We could see right through the open door, to a counter with a till, a table, two chairs. At the back was a sign marked 'restroom'.

'Carly, I need the loo. There's a toilet in there.'

'Go and pee in the woods,' she said. 'No way am I going inside.'

'Wait for me? I'll only be a second.'

'Just hurry, OK?'

I went into the office and through to the toilet. The door creaked open, like it hadn't been used for a very long time. Outside I could hear Carly calling.

'Hurry up, for God's sake, I'm getting really scared.'

The loo was reassuringly clean. I used it and washed my hands. There was a sudden bang. I jumped.

'Carly?'

No answer. The door to the restroom had slammed shut. I pushed at it, but it wouldn't open. I panicked.

'Carly? For God's sake, I'm stuck! Carly, where the hell are you?'

I hammered and hammered at the door, but it refused to budge. Somehow, it must have got stuck from the other side. I rifled through my bag to see if there was anything I could lever it open with.

Nothing. I banged on it again.

'Carly?' She must have gone back to the car and couldn't hear me. Then I noticed the window at the back of the toilet. It was small, but I thought I might just be able to get through it. It was open. Hands shaking, I climbed onto the toilet seat and onto the tank cover. My feet slipped, and I grabbed wildly for the top of the partition wall. With a heave, I hauled myself up to the window, my knee grazing painfully on the metal frame. I was there, and the air rushed towards me like a taste of freedom. Outside I could see the forest more closely. The tree branches reached towards the gas station as if trying to embrace it. The wind had got up and the branches swung wildly towards me. I scrabbled at the tiny window and managed to get myself half way through. It was a tight squeeze, but a good heave and I shot through it, falling awkwardly to the ground. I groaned. My ankle was twisted.

'Carly? Help!'

No reply. I got up and limped round the corner to the forecourt.

Carly was not there. Neither was the car. I couldn't believe it. Carly wouldn't go off and leave me here. We were best friends, had been friends for ages. No way would she abandon me alone in this freaky place. Maybe she saw a light somewhere and had gone for help. Anything. But she wouldn't have left me.

I turned round. It was windy. That must be it. Of course, that must be it, for I swore that the attendant had moved, was in a different place from when we arrived. The angle of his arms at the pump, something in the way he was standing…it had changed. Now I was seriously frightened. I went back into the building. Maybe there was a phone in there. My mobile had lost signal when we turned off the highway. And where the hell was Carly? I sat at the table and sobbed. I must have been there for a good hour, numb with fear, tears streaming down my face, but I couldn't tell what time it was, because my watch seemed to have stopped. And outside, oddly, the light was the same as when we had arrived, as if the day had somehow frozen in that moment. And then I realised.

A surreal painting, I'd thought when we arrived - and it was. I remembered what it reminded me of. A painting by Edward Hopper. I tried to imagine it. There was a gas station, the road ending, the light. But you couldn't see inside the gas station, couldn't see that there was a person in there, a girl sitting at the table. Trapped inside the painting.

UGLY AS SIN *and other clichés*

A Stitch in Time

Sue Wright

Ann extracted a needle from the depths of the pincushion where it was almost, but not quite, submerged. Only the eye, with its inch of bright pink thread, had made it visible. She pulled out the thread and dropped it onto the table alongside the scissors and the pair of grey trousers that lay in a rumpled heap next to the reel of sensible grey cotton.

She looked out of the window for a moment or two, remembering the fabric that she had once stitched so carefully with that pink thread. She could almost feel the contrast between the floating softness of honeymoon silk and the gritty dampness of sand on her bare feet. She shook her head at the grit of her married life; there had been more rough than smooth.

Turning to the task in hand, she rethreaded the needle with practised fingers and absent-mindedly knotted the end. Turning the trouser leg inside out, she carefully pulled out the remaining loose thread where the hem had come down. How careless her husband was, careless of his belongings and careless of her feelings. Each time she pushed her needle into the hem, she pulled at a thread of memory; a reminder of an insult or complaint. Living for years under his judgements, she had almost, but not quite, believed he must be right.

As she continued, feeling the regularity of the movement of her fingers, easing the fabric with her left hand, she regained just a little self-esteem, a sense of her ability with a needle and pride in the perfect evenness of the tiny pink stitches. With each stitch, the thread of her anger grew and the steel of her thoughts solidified. Her fingers moved faster and the needle stabbed the fabric ever more sharply as she went along. A particularly vicious movement jabbed at her finger and drew blood. With a sharp intake of breath she wiped the finger over the trouser leg, before finishing the hem and deftly snipping the thread.

She paused a moment, and then, driven by an energy she had all but forgotten, she worked on. The sharp blades of her best embroidery scissors cut this way and that, and delicate snowflake patterns began to emerge. With head on one side, she edged with blanket stitch, embellished with lazy daisy and fern stitches, interspersed with French knots. As a final flourish, she edged her work with beads, looped around the hem.

A little flushed, but otherwise calm, Ann tidied away her sewing things, hung the now magnificent trousers in the wardrobe, removed the credit card from the back pocket, and placed it carefully in her purse before leaving the house for the last time.

Better to Light a Candle than Curse the Dark

Dawn Wyndham

It was a revolt, that's what it was. What is it that pushes men over the edge of reason into the need to take heed, to take action, to take matters into their own hands? Wrongs crying out to be righted, grudges to be settled, pride to be satisfied? Whatever it is, it was at work in Drefach that summer.

As he walked to the village, the birds sang along with Benjamin, humming a hymn he'd learned at chapel. His younger brother Dafydd walked alongside, carrying a basket that was really too big for him to hold and slowed him down so that Ben had to stop and wait. He didn't mind. It was good to dawdle in the sunshine and throw stones into the river to pass the time. They'd been hard at work in the family weavers' shed, stamping on the cloth in large wooden half barrels to press the dye into the fleece. They all worked there, producing yarn and weaving cloth from the wool they got from their own sheep and sheep bought from other farmers around the Teifi Valley.

It was the income from this, together with the produce growing and sheep farming they did on their few acres of land, which provided the family with food and the means to survive. It wasn't a lot, but they didn't starve and, after two years of bad harvests, were better off than families who relied solely on farming for a livelihood.

At ten years old Ben considered himself quite grown up and an important member of the family business. He turned to see how far behind Dafydd was. He smiled at the sight of him, small for his eight years with a shock of dark hair like his own and a kerchief around his neck that matched his legs. Beneath his knee length breeches they were bright red up to the shins where they had stamped for hours in the coloured vats of water, side by side, making them both look like strange, bare-footed birds. His sisters would be up on the hills collecting plants for the dyeing; pokeweed berries, hibiscus flowers, red-purple daylilies, safflower and logwood. He knew what a good time they'd be having in the early summer sunshine foraging for dye plants and any edible fare they could find. His mouth watered at the idea that they may come across some wild strawberries or raspberries.

'Come on!' He called.

It was only half a mile to the village and the shop where their errand was taking them. One of the larger mill owners who used the family's services paid them in tokens that could only be spent at the mill-owned shop. It was dearer than the other store in the village, but they had no choice. Often the other smaller mills and the local farmers who bought their cloth paid in kind with things like coal, butter and potatoes. Even shoes on one occasion, but he only wore those to chapel and other Sunday meetings; most of the time he spent barefoot, like his brothers and sisters. They would be hand-me-downs for Dafydd soon if he kept growing like he did. He repeated the list their Mam had given them in his head. 'Two bags of flour, two bags of sugar, dried beans, salt, baking powder and cheese.' He sang it now to the tune of the hymn he'd been humming as he stood still and waited for Dafydd, nearly beside him.

'Two bags of flour, two bags of sugar, dried beans, salt, baking powder and cheese – la – la!'

'You're funny,' Dafydd laughed. 'You're clever too, to remember it all.'

Their father, Berwyn, had received a Bidding – an invitation to a feast following a wedding. The guests were encouraged to give the couple a present which would be repaid at an appropriate event such as the wedding of members of the giver's family. Mam was going to bake a cake. Their father, who was one of a very few who had been taught to read the scriptures by the minister of the Bethel Chapel, had read the invitation aloud to the family by candlelight when they were gathered for the evening meal last night:

'The intention of the bidder is this; with kindness and amity, with decency and liberality for the marriage of

Einion Owain and Llio Ellis, he invites you to come with your good will on the plate; bring current money; a shilling, or two, or three, or four, or five; with cheese and butter. We invite the husband and wife, and children and man-servants and maid-servants, from the greatest to the least. Come there early, you shall have victuals freely, and drink cheap, have stools to sit on, and fish if we can catch them; but if not, hold us excusable; and they will attend on you when you call upon them in return. Llanbadarn Fawr, 2nd June 1843.' It was signed *'Your humble and faithful servant, Titus Owain'.* Ben wondered why the owner of a much bigger farm and weaving shop should be a 'servant', let alone a 'humble' one, but the occasion was an exciting prospect and it was the first Bidding he could remember his family ever receiving. Now he was entrusted with the important task of buying ingredients for the cake. He mused on his responsibility and pulled himself up to his full height, proud he was trusted with it.

They turned right at the Sgwar y Gat where the toll gate was. There was an angry exchange going on between the farmer driving the cart (Ben could see it was their neighbour, Gwyn Lewis, at the reins) and the toll-gate keeper. This kind of altercation was happening more and more, on the rise again after the violence of the year before.

As always, the shop was crowded and busy both inside and out - and not just with shoppers. Almost as much as Sunday chapel, it was a place to meet; an opportunity to catch up with the latest village gossip, to do business and to advertise your wares, or to receive invitations and look for work.

For a village shop it was well stocked. Inside, it was lined with shelving along every wall, holding jars and bottles, boxes and pitchers. The slate floors were crammed with boxes, barrels, crates, and tables holding goods. The back wall was stacked high with sacks of dried fruit, flour, sugar, wheat and oats. The front counter held display cases for smaller items, as well as the machinery necessary for shop-keeping such as weighing scales for merchandise and a cash drawer.

The shopkeeper, employed by the mill owners, was Idris Jones, or Jones the Siop. A bluff, red-faced man with luxuriant pepper and salt sideburns and a very loud voice, he stood behind the counter, putting a small pack of yeast into a bag for a shy Mrs. Pryce, the minister's wife.

'Megan and me will be in chapel on Sunday,' he said solicitously. 'It's difficult to get there every week with her mother being ill the way she is.'

'How is she? Should I ask the minister to call?'

'No, no, diolch, this warm weather is a great help.' He looked at the numbers on a pad dangling from a string. 'That'll be two shillings and tuppence.'

She handed him some money and he opened the cash drawer.

Holding out some change he said, 'Give my greetings to the minister.'

Mrs Pryce smiled with a nod as she turned to leave. 'Hello boys,' she said as she saw Ben and Dafydd. 'Red today is it? I thought the river was running pink.'

'Yes,' said Dafydd, unnecessarily putting his leg out by way of proof. 'The rinsing's finished for today now.'

'I thought it made the Esgair look quite pretty,' she said. 'That's a big basket you're carrying.'

'We're here to buy things to make a cake for the Bidding,' said Ben, importantly. The wedding had been a buzz in the village for days now and Mrs. Pryce joined a conversation about it with a group of women nearby.

'So, young Ben, what can I get you?' Mr. Jones asked. Ben composed his face into what he hoped was a serious, business-like expression.

'I've got mill tokens. That's alright isn't it?' A nod from behind the counter and Ben launched into the list he had carefully held in his head. The queue mounted behind them as the goods were weighed and packed and finally most of them were in the basket on the counter. Ben was sure he'd remembered everything and was quite pleased with himself that it had gone so well. Jones pushed his pencil behind one ear.

'That'll be three shillings and eleven pence halfpenny.'

A moment of doubt stalled Ben from handing over the tokens. He didn't think he had that much.

Dafydd, oblivious, was eyeing up a jar of barley sticks at the end of the counter. After what seemed like minutes, fumbling in his pocket he emptied the tokens onto the corner, feeling the waiting shoppers' eyes on the back of his neck.

'You'll have to give something back,' said the shopkeeper, counting the tokens and leaning forward.

'Oh! Why is his voice so loud?' thought Ben trying to maintain some sort of dignity.

'The mill tokens have been put down in value since last week. Now, let's see what we can do…'

Ben was frozen in a silent plea. 'Not the cake things please, not the cake things. What about the wedding? What about not being able to take anything to it? What about my Mam?'

'Well, the cheese costs the most,' said Mr. Jones, removing it from the basket. 'Have you got any tokens?' He turned to Dafydd with his eyebrows raised. Dafydd, cowering behind Ben, shook his head while Ben blushed as red as his legs and looked down in shame, his pride gone with the cheese. 'No, still not enough.'

'How much do you need?' asked Mrs. Pryce, stepping forward.

Ben gathered himself and looked her in the eyes, lifting his chin. 'Dim diolch,' he said, still blushing but determined to defend his pride and stop the lump in his throat, which was threatening to steal his voice.

'Take something else.' Ben took the beans and held them out, even though he knew they were for supper that night. There were murmurs of sympathy from the other shoppers. Many of them were also suffering from the greed of the mill owners. Ben held his head high, giving Dafydd a big bag of sugar to carry and hurriedly left the shop. At least he'd managed to get the cake things for his Mam. He couldn't blame her; she wouldn't have known that the tokens' value had gone down. He just hoped she'd understand about the beans.

As they passed the Sgwar y Gat toll gate a cart trundled through in resentful silence.

Nobody knew who called the meeting in the barn of Gwyddyl farm on the Moelfre foothills and, apart from those present, nobody knew and nobody told who attended.

There was an air of resoluteness about them as they filed into the stall at the back. Despite the banter and camaraderie there was a sense of serious purpose to the gathering - the spirit of the countryside; young men ready to fight for their ideas, older men to fight for their families and every one of them ready to fight for their livelihoods. There were about fifty of them in all, farmers, farm labourers, mill workers, small mill owners, servants, small business owners and the minister. Even Jones the Siop was there. Gwyn Lewis, Iolo Thomas, Alun Pritchard, Einion Owain and his father, Titus; Berwyn Jones, Benjamin's father and Ben's two elder brothers, Bran and Tomas amongst them.

The crowded barn was lit with torches and candles, the light leaving bizarre puddles of dark shadow around the hay stalls and the men. Ewan Jones, the owner of the farm, stood at the front, next to him was Johnny Lewis, owner of a small but growing wool mill in the Cwmpengraig valley. Ewan's wife and daughters had just retreated from the barn, leaving behind a small barrel each of ale and cider and a couple of pitchers of elderflower cordial for those who didn't imbibe. The clay jugs glowed chestnut in the candlelight.

'Help yourselves boys,' said Ewan and they gathered round the drinks, finding the distraction a welcome release of tension as they teased each other about the ale.

'Steady now Einion, we don't want you falling asleep next to that new bride of yours.'

'Oh, I've always been partial to a good falling-asleep-next-to myself!' called a voice from the side.

'You'll be paying cheap for the fulling water tomorrow Adam!' Adam Evans worked for one of the mills, going round the village every morning collecting urine, an important ingredient for fulling cloth in the dying sheds. Abstainer's urine was worth twice as much because it was considered to be purer.

'Let's get started then,' called out Ewan Jones and they gathered round, quieter and full of attention, some standing, some sitting on bales of hay. 'We're all here because we've been suffering. True, I'll grant you, that the farmers have had the worst of it and the wool mills are keeping their heads above water - but only just.' There were murmurs of agreement. 'The Turnpike Trusts that operate the toll gates are getting greedier. The Lewes's up at Llynysnewydd Mansion, who own the land that our farms and mills sit on, have entered into a new agreement with the church trusts. There's word in the valleys that the tolls are going to rise again. It affects every single one of us.'

'The Lord knows what will happen to us!'

'Aye! They've closed some of the drover's lanes too!' It was a fact. One way the farmers and weavers got the sheep from the fields to other farms or the market and avoided going along a road was to drive them along 'green lanes', the narrow tracks of grass with high hedgerows either side that criss-crossed the countryside for miles around. One by one they were being blocked by felled trees or mounds of earth.

Iolo Thomas stepped forward. 'Three shillings is the price I paid at the kilns for a two-horse load of lime, and the tolls I paid cost two shillings from Carmarthen. That'll go up to four shillings and sixpence if they put in the new tolls at the prices they're talking about. I'll have to double my yield of corn to cover it – and the cost of grinding at Drefelin Grinding Mill is controlled by the Lewes's too.'

'Like us weavers too!' shouted Berwyn. 'We can't get to markets to sell our cloth without it costing us more than the cloth's worth sometimes.'

'They're bleeding us dry with tithes and tolls.'

'I've got to go to the kilns to buy lime to fertilise

that top field.'

'And take the wool shearing to the mills.'

The costs were highest in all the places they couldn't stay away from if they were to keep their farms and mills working and their families from starving.

'I know,' said Ethan Pryce, the minister, who resented the landlords and the formal Church of Wales as much as his parishioners. 'A new gate has been erected on the Parish road between Cynwyl Elfed and Cwmduadd and a new sixpenny toll for a horse and cart. A fortnight ago the bridge on the road to Drefelin was broken down by a flood and the Lewes's refused to do anything, so we parishioners had to get together to repair it – and the tolls are supposed to go towards the upkeep.'

He was hitting his stride now, driven by indignation and years of practice delivering sermons from the pulpit of the Bethel and Soar chapels. He could feel the support of the men gathering around him.

'The Good Lord knows it's getting out of hand. There's not a by-lane or track that a cart can reach the lime-kilns by that hasn't got a bar or a chain across it. If there's a lane by which one or two farmers can get to their farms without paying a toll, one of these blackguards makes an application to the trustees to grant a bar on it. There is never a fair held in any of the villages or towns but a toll contractor surrounds the town and every access to it with a cordon of toll-bars, so they catch every farmer who has cattle, or sheep, or horses, or carts to bring to the fair and every wool weaver who has cloth to sell. What's making it worse too, they're saying, is some of these chains are put across the lanes by crooks demanding tolls without any license at all!'

Angry conversations had broken out amongst the men. Dark mutterings of revenge and resentment were made all the worse by a feeling of impotence. Each one a victim of the power held over them by the land owners and the church.

'I won't be able to feed my family if it goes on much longer.'

'So, what are we going to do about it?'

'My Gwyneth is expecting our third soon. How am I going to feed them?'

'Are we ready to do something?'

'Aye!' came a roar from the gathered men. 'Aye!'

From the shadows at the back of the crowd a man stepped forward. No-one had noticed him before, despite the fact that he was taller and more heavily built than any man there. A ragged jerkin clothed shoulders and arms thick with muscle, his legs sturdy as a cart horse. His long auburn hair and whiskers added to his presence and the shouting died in a breath as he came to the front. He was a stranger, although strangely familiar. He certainly wasn't a local and nobody there had met him before, yet Johnny Lewis put out a hand to shake his, while Ewan Jones slapped the man on the back as he turned to address his neighbours.

'This,' he said, with a flourish, 'is none other than Gwilym Rees Jones.'

There was a buzz of excitement; Gwilym Rees Jones was known as a colourful character, devoutly religious, with a reputation for being outrageous. He was a regular reciter of the 'pwnc', the catechism of the points of the Scriptures in his local chapel on Whit Sunday, but it was his prowess as a prize fighter in fairs throughout the valleys that earned him extra respect.

'We need you all to give your word, to swear an oath, that what you hear from now on is held sacred and secret between us. Any man here feeling he can't do this must leave now and know that what follows here is no longer his concern, for fear of being cast out from his chapel.' Ethan was regarding them all sternly, holding up a large black bible. The blend of anticipation and fervour in the crowd held a low charge of menace.

'This is getting serious Da,' whispered Bran to Berwyn.

'I know son, but I'm here for us all. I shan't falter now, although you must make your own choice.'

At seventeen, Bran considered himself a man. He sometimes struggled though, being often in the shadow of his younger, but larger and stronger, brother Tomas. He glanced across at him now. He was bright-eyed and flushed with excitement, relishing the turmoil and passion that crackled in the air around them.

'We'll all stand together Da. I'll not be found wanting.' said Bran. His father responded with a squeeze of his shoulder and nod of assent. Not one man left the barn.

'We're going to bring out the Ceffyl Pren comrades.' shouted Gwilym Rees Jones in a voice loud as thunder. 'We're going to free ourselves from this tyranny! Just like the burning of the toll houses at Narberth and Llanelli and the destroying of the tollgate at Efailwen and gates all across the Preselis last year - we'll show the Trusts and landlords of Drefach our blackened faces and they will cower before us!'

They all knew the Ceffyl Pren, the Wooden Horse, in most cases not a horse at all, but a ladder or frame used to carry and humiliate a person to expose him for some great sin or disgraceful act. One or two of them had felt it at their own backs in the past. Nobody really trusted the justice of the gentry, the despised landowners and State, who believed that ownership of property afforded them special rights. Crimes against property were dealt with harshly, magistrates believing they had to protect their own interests, but issues of morality and honour were totally ignored.

Truth was that common law ruled much more fairly and with more immediacy than any of the official powers of justice, especially in these pious, moralistic small villages where everyone knew everyone else's business and the community was a cohesive whole. It wasn't uncommon for wife beaters, petty thieves, adulterers, young men refusing to marry girls made pregnant by them, or neglecting to support their illegitimate children to be taken from their houses late at night and tried by a jury of local men. Then, if found guilty, strapped to the Ceffyl Pren to be publicly beaten, usually with sticks, by the women of the village for extra shame.

It had been a tradition for generations, back hundreds of years and it had served them well. It was illegal, of course, so the 'Jurors' disguised themselves in women's clothes over their work clothes and blacked their faces. This lent an air of pantomime to proceedings and sometimes trials were even accompanied by songs and laughter, but there was always a grim purpose behind them, deep beneath the frothy surface, there was a serious and steadfast intent.

'We dressed as women again to attack the toll gates and houses, aye, and blacked our faces too,' admitted Gwilym. 'We were proud to be the men who brought justice to the villains who are fleecing us – and we will be again when we join together and march on the toll houses and gates hereabouts. Are you with us?'

Of course they had all heard about the riots and the burning of the toll houses and breaking down of the gates. They had all heard of Merched Beca, Rebecca's daughters, dressed as women and faces blacked. They had heard of other violence too, of toll-collectors being threatened that if they ever take a toll again, Rebecca will kill them, so that some of them refused to work for the Trusts for fear their houses would be burned down. The assembled men had all sympathised with the rioters, but never before been roused to strike at the tolls themselves. Now, though, it was different. Now it was time.

There was a resounding 'AYE!'

The Minister opened his bible, 'Genesis 24:60. They blessed Rebekah and said unto her, "Thou art our sister, be thou the mother of thousands of millions, and let thy seed possess the gate of those which hate them".'

Gwilym Rees Jones was standing on a hay bale now, a lighted torch held high above his head.

'I am Rebecca!'

The cheering broke out in earnest; loud and passionate, a mix of defiance and purpose. A wind blew through the throng that stirred heads to think and minds to dream that they could rid themselves of the oppressive burden of the tolls once and for all.

Ben, radiantly in his element, bustled to and fro, pushing, pulling, laughing and chattering as though it was his job to keep everyone's spirits up. Not that it was really necessary; there was an atmosphere of revelry, expectation and in some cases even jollity. They had chosen to meet at Yr Ogof, Berwyn's mill house, because of its proximity to the village. The cave that gave the place its name, half way up the hill behind it, was large enough to hide at least fifty men and the weaving shed, the fulling and dyeing room, and even the living quarters, were also crowded with men and boys. They must have been more than a hundred all told.

The plan was to march on the toll house at Sgwar y Gat, demand that the toll-keeper leave, and burn down the house and destroy the gate. There was to be simultaneous destruction of other toll gates and chains around Newcastle Emlyn – in Cynwyl Elfed, Cwmduadd, Langeler and Waungilwen. The word had been passed through the community at prayer meetings and chapel services, secretly whispered outside and inside Idris Jones' shop, shared in low tones at sheep markets and the lime kiln and between women as they spun the wool or worked at the looms. The hatred of the Tollgate Trusts had become a focus for all the ills and persecutions that they had suffered in recent times and feelings were running high.

'You look lovely, my dear,' twinkled Iolo to Bran, bowing low and reaching to kiss his hand.

'Get off with you!' said Bran, laughing. 'You're spoken for!' They were both wearing women's white nightgowns over their work clothes and each had on a mob cap, pulled incongruously down over their ears. Almost every man there was attired in women's clothes over their own, many also wearing mob caps. Looking part grotesque and part comical they all had their faces blackened with coal or charcoal, making the whites of their eyes and their teeth stand out in stark contrast. Rebecca's daughters, ready to fulfil the scriptures, to 'possess the gate of those which hate them'.

In the kitchen, women were gathered by the fire, also making preparations, but with heavier hearts. The logs in the fireplace shifted, releasing a collection of snaps and pops into the air. Ffion, Berwyn's wife, named after the foxgloves that turned the cloth a deep verdant green, was tearing strips from an old petticoat and rolling them into bandages. Her lips pursed in concentration, she put a prayer into each turn of her hand that there would be no serious use for the product of her task.

'We beseech you, Lord, that during this night violence will be tempered with reason and that, if love and peace withdraw from Drefach for a time, they won't travel too far.'

She looked across at Llio, Einion Owain's new bride, dipping torches into a vat of tar and stacking them on the dirt floor, and caught her eye. They smiled at each other, each knowing the fear that was in the other's heart and both understanding that it had to be so. The tolls had to stop. The other women were whispering comfort to each other in a song-voiced muttering, glances travelling from one to the next like a shudder.

Next door in the weaving room, men were filing past where Johnny Lewis and Ethan Pryce were handing out the few pistols they had. Each man chosen because he knew how to handle and load the weapons, each man under strict instruction to only fire them in the air. No-one wanted bloodshed. No-one really thought it would be necessary and that the downfall of the tolls would be noisy, even theatrical, but bloodless. There was a low refrain of chatter filling the room. Letting in a blast of night air, the door opened and Gwilym Rees Jones brought in a square box and Ethan opened it.

It was filled with cartridges and at the sight of them even the stoutest hearts quivered and there was a momentary silence. Ethan, smiling encouragement, passed them out; each man issued with just five cartridges each. It was a starless night. The invisible guardian of their secrecy and surprise, darkness, became a co-conspirator. As sometimes happens, nature seemed to have matched herself to the actions of men and there was a heavy mantle of cloud. They had all assembled in front of the mill, a large mob of men-at-arms in frocks. They each carried a weapon; a few of them rifles and pistols, but most of them scythes, pick-axes, sticks, cudgels, saws and hay-forks. Many also held aloft a torch or tallow candle, lighting the mob and shining orange in the dark, lending almost an air of carnival.

Gwilym Rees Jones was on horseback. 'Daughters, we are under the eyes of God and of our people. We are the tokens of our cause and our actions tonight must be brave and fair. We may see opposition, even battle, but let no man shed blood without cause and let us all fulfil our promise and hold to justice those who oppress us.' Someone handed him a flag.

If faith and will and anger were sounds, there would have been a cacophony. Instead, for stealth, they walked in silence; even the few excited boys like Ben who'd contrived to hide in the throng against their parent's warnings, ('I am ten after all...') The short walk to the village was made to the accompaniment only of men's breath, the fall of feet, the horse's hooves and the clanging and jangling of their weapons.

At the Sgwar y Gat toll house gate they came to a halt. It was very quiet, nothing stirred and the mob stood uncomfortably expectant.

They moved forward, jostling, shouting, raising their torches ready to throw. Just then the door to the toll gate opened and the toll-keeper, Iain Williams, appeared. A tall, extremely thin man, despised by the villagers, he wore a terrified mechanical smile, the result of too much jaw and too little flesh, displaying his teeth rather than his nature.

'Wait! Let me out first. I mean no-one any harm.' He held his arms aloft.

'Is there anybody else in there?'

As Iain shook his head Johnny Lewis grabbed him and passed him back to the mob. Now the way to destruction was clear. They surged forward, whooping, hollering, firing shots in the air as they put the toll house to the torch, breaking down the door, smashing the windows and pounding the wood of the gates to splinters. Cheering and shouting, lit by the flames, they vented their resentment and hatred on the stones of the house and bars of the gate. The flames grew higher and the smell of smoke palled over them as it rose to the sky.

The noise drowned out the thrumming at first. Then it became more distinct: The beat of hooves. Suddenly a drum beat the charge.

From the lane behind the shop a detachment of about forty of the 4th Dragoons arrived at a gallop with sabres drawn and bore down on the mob. It was a moment when the instinct for self-preservation cried out loud. The Rebeccas had been ready to fight body to body, hand to hand, with rough weapons and bare fists, but they all wanted to live and the mass of armed soldiers slashing long blades this way and that was irresistible. In noise and confusion the rioters panicked and scattered in all directions. Ben, in the heart of the melee, fell and was caught by the sabre of a passing dragoon. Tomos was next to him. He scooped him up and, not feeling the weight of his brother over his shoulder, ran for his life.

Back at Ogof Mill, most chilling of all was the silence, so sudden and final, as if all the world has paused to take a breath; yet only for a moment, and then the sounds trickled slowly back to life.

Berwyn held his son, handling him as though he feared to hurt him, noting that his body had a lightness he hadn't noticed before. Weeping quietly, Ffion knelt beside him and gently removed the boy's shirt as if tending his wounds now, binding them up with the bandages she had rolled just hours earlier could make a difference and bring him back. Berwyn held up his shirt so all could see its bloodstained holes.

A year later, Ffion sat alone at the big spinning wheel. The riots had stopped, but they hadn't been the redemption from poverty or the justice from an unfair system they thought they would be. The villagers had all been tight-lipped and neither the names of the leaders nor any of the rioters had been told, besides, the authorities seemed to have little appetite for pursuing prosecutions. The wool industry was taking off and that was what really made a difference to the village. Some rent reductions had been made and the hated toll on lime movement had been cut by half.

It all mattered little to her. They had buried Benjamin in the graveyard on top of the hill above the Soar chapel, behind the woods where he used to run with his dog, where he used to pick mushrooms and bluebells, where the sky is as wide and bright as his smile. After the funeral, as was customary, they had put his shoes in the thatch above the sleeping platform. It was a comfort that he was somehow still here near the hearth.

As she spun, Ffion hummed the hymn that was his favourite.

Outside the window the birds sang along.

A Little Knowledge

Dawn Morgan

Eliza looked at her new companion with amusement. Ever since Kurseong station, on their climb through the Himalayan foothills, William Hall had been shaking his head from side to side, occasionally batting it with his palm, like a bear with an insect trapped inside its ear.

'You'll feel better when we rise higher,' said Eliza, curving her lips. 'It's the ascent that causes the difficulty. As soon as you feel an explosion in your ears, all will be well.'

William looked far from comforted by her words: his face became such a picture of alarm that it drew a laugh from Eliza and her brother.

'Don't let her frighten you,' said George, stretching comfortably beside his sister in the open railway carriage. 'It will be a mere 'pop'. You'll barely notice.'

William, sitting opposite, had been hunched miserably all through their journey from the Bengal plains. He had taken to chewing his lips whenever the carriage shuddered or the canvas roof shook, which happened often. At every hiss or sputter of the steam engine, he would sit forward in his seat, as if preparing to escape into the jungle.

Eliza sat with her arm reclined along the side of the carriage and looked at him. She was not in the habit of giving her good opinion easily, so she was surprised to find that in the case of Mr Hall – and without any firm decision on her part – it was already bestowed. Yet she knew nothing about him except from his own account – he was travelling to visit his aunt at the sanatorium in Darjeeling – and from the quiet manners he'd displayed since they all boarded the train as strangers in Siliguri. For a few moments, she watched the green landscape reflected in the circles of his spectacles. Then she gave a soft laugh as William gripped the edge of his seat in response to a screeching sound and the backsliding motion of the carriages.

'Good God! We're descending!' he said, craning his neck towards the valley.

George laughed and remained easy in his seat, his legs stretched out in front him.

'Personally,' said George, 'I have always preferred travelling in reverse. But don't be alarmed,' he added. 'It's just a temporary check. In my experience, the average direction of this conveyance is upwards.'

'They are sanding the track,' explained Eliza. 'It is quite routine. If you look to the front, you will see them.'

William turned his head and poked it cautiously into the sunshine. He could see along the length of the train where it curved around the contour of the mountain. Two small boys were scattering sand immediately in front of the engine, which soon began to ascend again. He smiled as he drew back his head. Eliza matched his smile with an expression of great warmth.

Their conversation grew more informal as they rose through the hills, stopping often to take tea while the engine took on water. When they passed Sonada station, the hills became wrapped in clouds, which clung around them in a cool layer. As if by agreement, their voices grew softer and their words less frequent in that white, subdued world; and it seemed to Eliza that their companionship bloomed in the mist.

'Shall we see your estate?' asked William, towards the end of their journey. He looked out at the slopes that were now looming into view through the dispersing cloud. Eliza shook her head.

'Our place is several miles to the east. But the landscape is similar to this.' She nodded at the rows of cultivation softening the hillsides.

'You shall come tomorrow,' said George.

'I must see my aunt first,' said William.

'Yes, and then you will come.'

William nodded. He barely needed the invitation. There was such easiness between the three of them, by the time the train pulled into Darjeeling, that it would have been astonishing if they hadn't arranged to be together again, as soon as they could, at the roof of the world.

William was dusty and weary when he clambered from his hired carriage the following day. The last few miles of road had been rough, and he had been thrown from his seat on two occasions. The white bungalow on its green slope had the air of a refuge. Its windows and doors stood open to the evening, and the heat was pleasantly moderate – no more than he'd endured on a summer afternoon at his father's house in Surrey – and the air was clean after a rain storm, allowing a humbling view of Mount Kanchenjunga. As he approached the front steps, he made out a white shape on the veranda.

'I'm taking tea,' said George. 'Come on up.'

William took a seat in the shade and placed his hat on an empty chair while George poured tea.

'Eliza's gone off with her sketchbook,' said George, nodding towards the garden below, where a red bonnet was visible in the foliage. 'I expect she'll join us when she's thirsty. Sugar?'

William shook his head and took the offered cup.

'This is a beautiful place,' he said, gazing up at the peaks, which rose in a silent mass behind the blue-washed foothills.

'Yes, it has its moments,' said George. 'Though I hardly notice it these days.'

'Eliza does,' said William, glancing towards the garden.

'Yes. Eliza does.'

William found the tea pleasantly fresh and said so.

'Rain tea,' said George.

'You make it from rainwater?'

'No,' laughed George. 'It's harvested in summer, during the Monsoon. The First Flush is our best, picked in April, but Eliza prefers our summer crop. She says it tastes of rain, which is fanciful...'

'I think so too!' said William.

'Nonsense,' said George, affably. 'It's just tea. The finest there is, of course: *sinensis*, the true China leaf. I can't say I like the home-grown *assamica*, which tastes rather too much of soil for my taste.'

William had no opinion on the matter and remained silent, looking out across the shrubs to the red bonnet.

'You like her, don't you?' asked George, after a companionable pause.

'Of course. How could I not?'

George leaned forward and took a cube of sugar from the bowl, dropping it into his cup.

'You've heard of the scandal, of course.' George spoke in a light tone, but his face was alert.

'What do you mean?'

'The fellow from Siliguri.'

'What fellow?'

'Oh, I was sure the story would have reached you, through your aunt,' said George, stirring his tea. 'It was quite the favourite subject, for a time. She went off with some Indian fellow, dragging a bunch of sherpas behind them.'

'What fellow?' William's voice was hard.

'I forget his name. A guide, according to Eliza. She followed him for months, up mountains and down rivers. Sent back articles to Calcutta and London. Had a few published, at the time.' George shook his head, 'But it has never quite left her.'

William put his cup back in its saucer and placed it on the table. He stared unhappily towards the garden.

'I'm sorry to break it to you, old fellow,' said George. 'But I'm sure you'll agree it's better to know. And far better that you hear it from us.'

'From you,' said William, his voice drained of all warmth.

'Oh Lord. This has quite ruined the afternoon.' George rang a bell on the table. 'I do believe it will rain. Shall we have some brandy, while we can still sit out?'

William rose from his seat without answering and went down to the garden. When he reached the bench where Eliza's sat, he waited silently, casting his shadow across her sketchbook.

'He has told you, then?' said Eliza, without looking up.

William gazed at her head but was silent. She continued to sketch.

'I thought he might,' she said. 'He likes you very much.' She glanced up at him. 'Did you know that?'

'Is it true? About the fellow from Siliguri?'

'Does it matter?'

William drew a breath through his nose and thrust his hands in his pockets. Eliza sighed and put down her sketchbook.

'I don't believe I did anything wrong,' she said, her eyes on the mountains. 'I travelled with a guide. He was called Amit. He was a good man.'

'And that is all?'

'That is all.'

'I can trust you in this?' William's voice quavered.

She said nothing, but she looked at him with such frank simplicity that William, with all the yearning in his fearful, honest heart, took it for purity and threw himself on his knees in front of her.

When they returned to the bungalow in the half-light, they could see the red tip of a cigar burning on the veranda.

'It keeps the mosquitoes away,' said George, blowing out smoke and glancing at their entwined hands. 'Should I order champagne? Or shall we toast the occasion with tea?'

That evening, William watched Eliza with an exhausted rapture. As he traced her movements in the dusk, his blood slushing in his head, he pushed away all discordant thoughts. His lips moved in silent praise as he enjoyed the fineness of her profile, her elegant posture, the beautiful way she bent her neck to sip her tea, like a swan dipping its beak into a river.

And he hadn't the faintest premonition that all her manners – from her languorous stooping to the way she crooked her fingers around a tea cup – would one day fill him with distaste.

UGLY AS SIN *and other clichés*

Still Waters Run Deep

Sal Starling

He dropped to his knees at the water's edge and watched the small ripples lazily slip back and forth across its muddy rim. His racing heart gradually slowed to the rhythm of their pulse. Scanning the smooth sheet of water he wondered if the world would somehow be different now. He looked around.

A flurry of ducks smacked their wings as they pushed away from the lake, and spangles of water cascaded from their feathers like summer rain.

Perfect halos radiated across the water's surface where trout rose to snatch skating insects.

A cacophony of crickets chirruped through tall grasses fringing the lake's boundary, just out of its grasp. And cotton clouds hung in the afternoon sky, waiting for a breeze to carry them to cooler lands where they would weep away their existence.

Nothing had changed.

He leaned forward on all fours to look into the crystal water. A face gazed back, young and unshaven. Droplets of sweat trickled from his dishevelled fair hair, and lips parted in the trace of a smile.

The reflection was familiar, but he knew it was someone else; someone with eyes as empty as a pit. He slid his hands into the face to see it warp and drift away.

He slowly rubbed his fingers together in the cool, cleansing water. New ripples formed and undulated across the surface, gently swirling the blood into soft clouds of sunset red.

When Push Comes to Shove

Dawn Wyndham

The story you are about to read is true. Not even the names have been changed. Why bother? To protect the innocent? There were no innocent …

I like being a private eye and even though, once in a while, I've had my gums massaged with an automobile jack, the sweet smell of money makes it all worth the trouble. Not to mention the dames.

What I do for a living may not be very reputable, but here - in the Deep South? Down these mean streets a character must go who isn't himself mean. Who is carefully constructed, neither tarnished nor afraid. I like to think that I have a sort of honour written into my character, by instinct, by inevitability, without thought of it. Unlike some. It certainly doesn't flow with the genes, if my brother is anything to go by.

The name's Dick. You can find me in the phone book under T.

TWEEDLE, D. Private Investigator.

It was a night like any other. I was on my way to the barber's store; it's important for a character to be well groomed. I like to think I'm a snappy dresser. I was wearing the check trousers, yellow blazer and bow tie that are my hallmark. I try to stay slim, but I struggle. I guess I must have just been drawn fat. I wear a school cap. It's an affectation, I know, but I think it shows class. Upper third grade to be precise.

I'd had the usual row with my twin brother, Dumitri, Dum for short. Dum by name and dumb by nature. God! He can act like such a shit. Copying me in everything I wear, the same trousers and blazer, only his was blue. Always following me, although he's been able to do it less and less since I learned how to shake off a tail.

Talking of dames, it's been forever since I last hung out with that young tootsie, Alice. Her call came out of the past, leaping from the page onto my cell phone. It had been years.

'Dick?'

'Yeah, Dick Tweedle, Private Investigator at your service.'

'Dick, it's Alice,' a pause, 'you remember me?'

Wow! This IS a surprise. I'd thought about her and wondered how she'd matured since that once upon a time.

'Could we meet? There are some things I have to tell you.'

I looked up from my coffee as she turned the corner, her long blonde hair flying behind her in her rush to get inside. It had been snowing since the top of the last page.

We shook hands rather formally. We'd arranged to meet in a diner, since I'm having my umpteenth stab at giving up the liquor. My, my, how she's grown. She's become a talkative, charming and quintessentially English upper-crust eccentric. Ignoring the childish pinafore dress and striped stockings, I took in details of her as she chattered breathlessly on. She dabbles in Freud, toxicology, and British folklore. She's skilled at chess, croquet, poetry and dagger-throwing. I looked her up and down. Not bad. I drank in her perfume. She sure smells good too. She's fit, although she definitely knows it, judging by the amount of time she spends in the mirror.

'What did you want to tell me?' I eventually managed to interrupt her.

'Where do I start?' she asked.

'Just the facts, ma'am, I'm only working the day shift.'

'I've learned the truth about Mr. Dumpty. He didn't fall, he was PUSHED.'

I sat back. Ah, Humpty Dumpty. I had never forgotten him. I had tried to befriend him, get him out of his shell. I had often wondered why Henrietta and Cockburn Dumpty hadn't had the good sense to call their offspring something more sensible, like Gary or Cockburn Junior. No wonder he got bullied, he was an easy target and not just for his name. Every egg is yellow inside.

I remembered the day it happened. He was sat

high on the wall. Stupid place to sit if you're an egg. I recall all the king's horses and all the king's men turning up. Don't know why it had to be all of them for what good they did. They had no idea how to re-construct him. It was such a mess. They'd have been better off calling Faberge.

'How do you know?' I asked her. 'And why now, after all this time?'

'I only found out what happened yesterday. I called you as soon as I knew. I was mixing some potions in my toxicology laboratory for Snowy White – you know, the twitchy big-eared Angoran who was always late?'

I nodded.

'Well, I thought I'd try to make him a prescription that slowed time. I was so pleased with it I took some, thinking I would never again be in the dreadful hurry he was always in.'

'And?'

She was shaking, twiddling her blonde hair around her finger distractedly.

'I overdid the formula proportions and reversed time instead of just slowing it down. I sent myself into the past. I found myself back at the wall, seconds after it happened. Dick - I saw someone I thought was you running away. He had on the same trousers and a pale blue blazer. Then I saw it: The speech bubble floating to the ground, a word balloon.'

I sat forward. Alice was on to something. 'What did it say?' I asked, trying to sound professionally casual.

Alice was leaning forward too. I could feel her breath on my cheek as she spoke, our faces almost touching.

'It said, *"Don't push me off Dum. I'll pay. I'll do anything. Please Dum, please don't push me! AAAaaaarrrggggghhhh!"'*

'I saved the bubble. I've still got it. It's proof he did it.'

I sat back. This was the plot twist I'd hoped for. I'd always known he was the other side of me. A twin, but the opposite - the bad reflection. Now I could rid myself of him at last.

'Can you bring me the word balloon to take to the cops?'

She frowned, 'Yes, I can, but it will cost you.'

I looked her in the eyes. She must have known I had little I could pay with. She was blushing.

'Cost me what?'

'Your silence about me. I just have to tell somebody.'

'What about you?'

A grin like a Cheshire cat lit her face. 'It was me who stole the tarts.'

The snow had turned to rain as I walked back to my office. A guy stopped me as we passed on the sidewalk.

'Say, have you got a light Mac?'

He held up a cigarette.

When Push Comes to Shove

I chortled,
'No, but I've got a bright yellow blazer.'

(With apologies to Lewis Carroll)

Out of the Woods

Sue Wright

A sound ripples down my back. Now, the words come in multiples, shrill or smooth, with or without pauses and the deepest of them rumbles around my feet. A door hinge creaks and more voices enter on a blast of cold air. The door slams and the volume rises. Now they come in waves, reverberating through me. How they could hear each other in the middle of the din, I have no idea. My solid carcass absorbs it all. I have known worse in my time, but then, I have been transformed more than once, before I came to be here in this pub. I remember the sounds of the outside world, carried on the wind; from the whisper of snowfall to the howl and crack of a storm. I was well rooted then and could bend and sway.

I was slow to reach my adult size, there were setbacks. I suffered all manner of stinging and biting insects, fought diseases, and withstood many a knock without losing my balance. My kind is known for their stability and strength. We looked out for each other in the bad winters and shared moisture in the long dry summers. It was the way of things. Year after year, decade after decade, we rubbed along together. We had responsibilities too, we supported others. We provided shelter in winter and shade in summer, nesting places, food. My family is high minded. We take the long view.

It must have been more than a hundred years before the first of my neighbours died. Then they went, one by one, winter by winter until I was the only one left to support the youngsters growing below. It left me vulnerable of course. When we had clustered together, our combined weight and strength fought off the worst onslaughts. Now by myself, I had to take it alone, which I did pretty well for the most part. But during one especially fierce winter storm I finally lost my footing. My relationship with the earth that had been strong for all my life had gone awry and I fell. It was a long way down and I lay there winded for months, maybe years.

When they came to get me, it didn't take them long to carve me up. The sound of the chainsaws was like the biggest swarm of wasps you ever heard, and I have hosted a good few wasps' nests in my time, I can tell you. I used to let them have a space in the crook of one of my branches and in return they discouraged the animals that liked to pick at my bark.

After my fall, it was a strange and very different world that I experienced, restful in a way. I suppose I was coming to recognise that I had had enough of holding my aged body upright when all my peers were gone. The foresters pared away my uppermost growth, tidied up the exposed roots. They reduced my girth and planked my length and I was no longer whole.

I lay in pieces, in the dark, for many months, 'seasoning' they called it. It made me laugh. If only they knew how many seasons I had already lived through. Eventually I was bought and carried off to a workshop where I was hewn, split, shaved and generally manipulated by means of cuts and joints into a piece of furniture. Not that I wasn't taken care of mind you, I was treated lovingly and my whorls and lines were much admired. Indeed, they were deemed to be enhanced by hours of smoothing with fine sand then polished with wax from my old friends the bees.

Did I tell you about the carving? Oh yes, there were embellishments too, here and there, intricate shapes and cuts. They itched a bit but I quite liked the effect in the end. People used to run their fingers over it, reminded me of the wind in my branches, back in the old days, not unpleasant.

I was settled in the church along with all the others. We were lined up in rows for the congregation to rest their backsides on. Oh dear, those backsides; anything from wriggling small ones to enormous heavy duty ones that squelched when they moved. Good job I was robust. The resonances there were more uplifting though. There was a soft energy to it that rolled through me. Although some singers were unable to hold a tune, somehow the whole thing hung together in a pleasant enough fashion.

After a couple of centuries of this, the glory days of the church declined and the pews began to empty. There were fewer people each week until eventually the vicar retired and they closed the church. It was cold and dull and quiet then, apart from the mice scuttling and scratching and the woodworm grinding their jaws. I didn't suffer them too badly, unlike some of the others.

The builder that eventually bought the place doused us all in some vile liquid to kill them off. It nearly killed me off too, nasty stuff. Then there were months of being stood on, used as a saw bench, covered in paint spatters and generally treated rather badly and then the builder's girlfriend decided to paint me purple. I took it as a bit of a come down as you might imagine.

Anyway, when they split up and went their separate ways, I was sold on to this pub. They rubbed all the paint off again and returned me to the good solid wood that I am. My back is against the wall now and I suffer the indignity of being slopped with beer and half-heartedly wiped down, I am often sticky. I acquiesce these days, just let the months and years roll by without paying much attention.

The next thing I knew there was a great upheaval, a massive fight one Saturday night. Bottles were thrown, blood was spilt, lots of it. That was a new one on me. I was badly damaged in the process, kicked to pieces, my ancient joints prised apart and left hanging loose. After the clearing up, the owner went out of business.

Reduced to a pile of broken wood, I was relegated to the bonfire. Stacked up against an old sofa and half a kitchen cupboard, dripping with petrol, I was facing the end, my old carcass turned to ashes. After the fire, it was oblivion for decades. I didn't mind that, the timescales of trees are long. Eventually, my essence was fully absorbed into the soil and I was taken up by a tiny seedling. We are one and the same now. My new consciousness has only just begun and I am trying to regain the old memories at the same time as relearn the basics from scratch.

A woman and child dug me up to plant in their garden. Here I am now, still barely as tall as a dandelion so she had to explain to the little boy that I would grow into a great big tree. He looked doubtful and I wished I could have told him about my lifetimes. That's what started me telling my story. Fortunately some of my old friends who were made into wood pulp have been able to help. So, here it is, out of the woods and onto paper.

UGLY AS SIN *and other clichés*

Shrinking Violet

Kathy Miles

It had started last year. Twelve months, two days, three hours and forty-nine seconds ago. She knew the exact time, because she had recorded it in her diary. 'Today I am shrinking.' It wasn't the usual kind of thing she wrote. Normally it would be 'went to town and met Mandy for a coffee' or 'Put the rubbish out. Next door's cat threw up on the carpet. Arthritis is bad this morning.' Everyday, boring stuff. But back then, the world was still its proper size.

She had first noticed it when she tried to retrieve a recipe book from the kitchen shelves. A bit of a stretch, but if she stood on tiptoe and yanked the corner, it would usually fall into her hands. That day, she couldn't reach it. Going on tiptoes was always problematic, but not impossible. Except that the shelf was now a good six inches away, and in the end, she had to fetch a small stepladder to get the book down. She wasn't particularly alarmed; it was just one of those things, and since the operation she'd already become used to the fact that her muscles had a mind of their own.

But then it was the shelves in the walk-in cupboard, where her best woollen sweaters were folded away for the winter . She needed the blue one embroidered with red ivy leaves, because she was going to meet a friend in town, and it went nicely with her navy trousers. She'd tidied the shelves over the summer, stacked everything in rows with no problem at all. Now, she couldn't even touch the edge of the shelf with her fingertips.

The shrinking continued. Sometimes it seemed to accelerate, and she'd suddenly find the shower controls were too far away, or the windows too high to clean. At other times it slowed, and she'd go through several weeks where she could grasp the things she needed without too much effort. But then it would start again without warning. After six months, climbing onto the step of a bus was a Herculean task. The bus drivers would offer a helping hand, thinking that she – now only four foot tall and dressed in a child's anorak – was an unaccompanied minor. Then they'd see her face, the wrinkles and white hair, and recoiled, as if she was some slow-witted troll that had ambled onto the bus from the pages of a story-book.

Nine months on, she rarely left the house. The internet was a great leveller, a place where she could have as much heft as she wanted. For who on Facebook cared that she was an 80 year old woman who measured only three foot from the top of her head to her toes? But that was yesterday. She hadn't dared to measure today, because the size 4 jeans she'd ordered last week were already spilling over the ends of her feet.

It would have been sensible, she sometimes thought, if she'd gone to the doctor when all this started. Perhaps he had some magic pill to stop it in its tracks. But there was always the fear that she wasn't actually shrinking at all. That it was all in her head. Scenarios stalked her dreams, visions of mental hospitals, homes for the demented, places that would restore her height but take away her freedom.

And there were some advantages to being little. Soon, she was able to crawl into the smallest spaces, inaccessible corners of the house that had been neglected for years and were full of accumulated dust. She gave all of them a really good clean. There was also the company. Insects, spiders, the odd mouse or two – she didn't dare think rat, though their tails were longer than she'd have liked – the scurrying beetles. She'd say a cheery 'Good Morning' to them each day, and was delighted when they greeted her in return. Of course, she was no longer able to use the oven or the fridge, but there were plenty of crumbs on the floor, and once she could squeeze through the crack in the front door, she found the pavement was rich with discarded food. But it was dangerous outside. She was in constant fear of being trodden on, and on one occasion, narrowly avoided being eaten by a passing dog. Cats, too, were risky, and she didn't want to be dragged ignominiously through the nearest cat-flap to become the plaything of some pampered Siamese.

She knew, of course, how it was going to end. She'd become a speck of dust, a

particle, and eventually, would stop existing. The thought didn't bother her. For now she was tiny, there was no more pain from the pesky arthritis; little as she was, she could skip and dance and jump, and her inch-long limbs were as flexible as a five year old's. And she never regretted the day, which seemed so very long ago, when she swigged back the contents of that small dark bottle marked 'Drink Me'.

What Goes Around, Comes Around

Sal Starling

'Surely goodness and mercy shall follow me all the days of my life, and I will dwell in the house of the Lord forever.'

A dry-eyed woman blew her nose into a paper tissue while flicking through the pages of 'Hymns Old and New'. Across the aisle sat a thin man, hunched and motionless - his grey overcoat, hair and pallor rendering him almost invisible in the dimly lit church. He gazed blankly into a space beyond the naked coffin laid at the feet of an angst-ridden Christ.

On the back pew perched two serial mourners, their tartan shopping trolleys parked beside them. With handbags clasped beneath overhanging bosoms, and scarves tied under sagging chins, they click-clacked humbugs around plastic teeth and speculated on the age of the deceased and cause of death.

Occasionally glancing through the open doors to see if it had stopped raining, they discussed the possibility of finishing their shopping and having a cup of tea and a scone before popping back for a wedding at 3.30pm.

'Blessed are those who mourn, for they will be comforted.' The minister glanced at his watch and offered his condolences to the meagre gathering before sliding into the vestry to memorise names for his 3.30 wedding.

By avoiding the town and taking the dual carriageway, the hearse driver was able to make the journey from church to crematorium in fifteen minutes. Heavy cloud, the coffin's only follower, rumbled across the afternoon sky and spat on all below.

Services at the crematorium had finished for the day, giving the undertakers unhindered access to wheel in their latest offering. The assistant duly signed relevant forms and checked details before wheeling the deceased through the back door to await the arrival of the technician.

The crematorium technician arrived ten minutes later. He shook the rain from his umbrella, hung up his coat, smoothed back his thin, damp hair and walked towards the new arrival. He pulled out a pair of horn-rimmed glasses, wiped away their mist with a faded handkerchief and leaned over to inspect the inscribed plate on the chest of the coffin.

'Grace ... Delly,' he whispered, slowly, deliberately.

The technician took his job very seriously, always ensuring the name followed the deceased at every stage of processing to ensure families took home the correct remains. On the computer he carefully checked and typed out the deceased's name and date of birth, *'Grace Phyllis Delly 14/08/1954'*, before printing it on a small white card. He placed the card beside the brass plate on top of the faux-mahogany coffin.

The cremation chamber had been working flat out all morning (February was always a busy month) and would quickly reach the optimum temperature of 975 degrees Celsius. While his assistant held open the door, the technician rolled the heavy wooden box feet first from the gurney into the mouth of the chamber, removing the newly printed card as it passed. The card was slid into a slot on the furnace door and checked once more.

'Grace ... Delly.'

Combustion takes between one and half to three hours, depending on body mass. Grace Delly was going to take the full three hours.

The technician observed progress through a fist-sized hole in the insulated door. As usual, the laminated coffin burned quickly, followed by soft tissue and organs which vaporised and made their escape through the chimney. Grace Delly's bones were the last of her to break down, displaying many shapes and forms on their journey to ash; exposed ribs took on the appearance of a tanker skeleton, and shrivelled arms, contorted by heat, rose towards the ceiling of the oven before falling to dust. Her blackened skull slowly slid back to reveal glowing empty sockets which glared heatedly at the spy-hole spectator.

While waiting for Grace Delly to cool down, the technician sat alone in the generated warmth to eat cheese and pickle sandwiches washed down by sweet, milky tea from his thermos flask. He filled the remaining empty minutes with his hobby of gluing matchsticks together to make intricate trinket boxes. He nodded a silent goodbye as his assistant swung open the back door to head off home - leaving behind a cold chill that swept away the last traces of heat. The technician put the final touches to his finest piece of work yet - a hinged box inlaid with mother-of-pearl buttons in the shape of a dove - and daydreamed about his imminent retirement and of spending longer hours in his little shed, carving, cutting and creating more beautiful things such as this.

Through the observation hole he checked the fragile framework of ashen bones before moving to the next stage. The label was carefully removed from the cremator and slipped into a slot on a small door below the furnace - where Grace Delly's remains fell after being raked, scraped and brushed through the grill above. Her detritus was then swept from the lower chamber, taken to the cremulator and emptied into the machine - the accompanying label confirming correct procedure,

'Grace ... Delly,' he said to no-one.

Satisfied that all was as it should be, the technician switched on the machine and watched impassively as she was thrown around the tumbler, her remains thrashed and beaten by a metal ball to reduce her to the texture of granulated coffee. The white label followed her to the final stage of processing where latex-covered fingers rummaged, and a large magnet sifted through her granules to remove all metal. Her blackened scrap was laid out neatly across the technician's bench. He removed his gloves and silently reviewed the leftovers.

There were tiny remnants of an oval wedding ring which had remained on the dead Grace Delly because her fingers, along with the rest of her, had grown obese and sausage-like through years of gorging herself on chips, curry, Guinness and chocolate. Frequent back-handers across the heads of her husband and children had contributed to the altered shape of the ring.

Fused black fragments of silver were all that remained of the nicotine-stained teeth once housed in a mouth that screamed abuse and obscenities at anyone who crossed her.

And finally, four steel suspenders - which had attached black fishnet stockings to the huge red corset she liked to wear before demanding sex from her husband, or any other man she could intimidate or coerce.

Her pacemaker had been removed before committal, negating the consensus of opinion that Grace Delly had no heart.

The technician poured her into a large plastic

container, screwed on the lid, and sellotaped the white card to the tub. After pushing up his tie and pulling on his overcoat, he tucked Grace Delly into his insulated lunch bag and left the building.

The charred bench overlooked a deserted park of burned and vandalised play equipment. Beyond its broken perimeter rose a bridge across a stinking, litter-filled canal. The technician smoothed a plastic carrier bag across the wet bench, sat down, and poured the last cup of tea from his flask before carefully unfolding and scanning the details on a sheet of pink paper. Grace Delly sat on the dirt between his feet. Little swirls of misty breath danced into the dusk as he mouthed the words,

'Advance Funeral Wishes of Grace Phyllis Delly ... It is my final wish to ... wicker coffin ... blue evening dress ... non-religious service ... horse-drawn hearse ... past the Spotted Cow pub and Delta Bingo ... burial at Woodleigh cemetery ... black marble headstone in the shape of a heart.'

He picked up the brown tub, carried it to the canal bridge and unscrewed the top. Scrunching up the sheet of paper in his boney fist, he stuffed it in the tub and replaced the lid.

Arthur Delly, crematorium technician, gave one final glance at the small white label,

'Grace ... Delly,' and dropped her into the cold, filthy mire below.

The Boot is on the Other Foot

Sue Wright

The upper was coming away from the sole along the instep where the foot that had once filled it had been too broad for comfort. The heel was heavily worn on one side and the surface of the toecap was scuffed and badly scraped. The lace was not fastened, but trailing loose and the tongue flopped out sideways onto the ground. The boot had evidently suffered neglect for several months before it ended up on this piece of ground, parted from its wearer for good.

Almost completely hidden from view, it lay on its side amongst the grasses and shrubs that grew alongside the track. This narrow strip of wilderness grew lush and high because apart from an annual blast from a propane torch to keep the edges within bounds, it had been undisturbed for decades. Late summers saw the release of a million dandelion seed heads. Each passing train brought in its wake a wind that drove them aloft and sent them gently on their way to colonise the ground beyond the verge.

On the allotments that thrived beside the railway track, the gardeners could be heard bemoaning the constant flurry of wafting seeds with their tiny canopies of down. These intrepid men worked the soil in all weathers and mostly wore the same tweed jackets and flat caps, regardless of the temperature. They were methodical in their actions; they took time to relish the chivvying of a hoe around seedlings, took satisfaction in the sharp slice of a spade into soil, or smiled at the sun during a moment of wiping a sweaty brow with the back of a hand. They wore old fashioned leather boots with good strong soles that kept their feet steady, even in the mud that sometimes persisted after frequent rain.

These were men who knew a thing or two about making and mending as well as growing. Their gnarled fingers were as dexterous as their minds. Old wooden window frames bartered from local builders, were made into cold frames with wooden sides that had once had pride of place in someone's lounge as a favourite sideboard or coffee table. When two or three greenhouses suffered the worst of a winter gale, they were painstakingly reconstructed with the addition of frosted windows reclaimed from skips. One shed was constructed from a grand Victorian wardrobe and had finials on the roof ends to rival a gothic cathedral and boasted a stained glass window that had once graced a suburban front door.

The men were a hospitable bunch in the main. They boiled water on ancient Primus stoves, brewed strong black tea in old cracked tea pots, and stirred powdered milk into old tin mugs that only occasionally got rinsed under the single tap at the far end of the allotment site. The passengers on the six o'clock from Paddington flashed past too fast to notice these gentlemen who leaned on their spades to chat over a shared pot of tea; and the men merely paused their conversation until it was out of earshot.

They were competitive though and liked to measure their own competence against their neighbour's under the guise of admiring each other's produce. It was, however, the least talkative one of their number who regularly produced the biggest, most flavoursome, vegetables and the sweetest, most prolific, fruits. It must have been some quirk of fate that endowed him with green fingers, or so they believed.

His presence was as familiar to the rest of them as a bean pole. Like a scarecrow, he was there, his worn clothes flapping in the wind, his hat pulled down so the peak shaded his eyes. He was tall and lanky, and walked with an angular ungainly stride, though his movements were spare and purposeful. They found him stand-offish and avoided intruding on his self-imposed privacy. Where once he had been known to give a curt good morning it had been years since anyone had heard him speak, so they never knew that he had become increasingly deaf as the years went by.

It was cool in the early morning as he made his way towards the allotment. As he had done many times before, he opted for the short cut across the track where the glittering mist deposited pearls of dew on the broad leaved plants along the verge. A troublesome stone had edged its way into his boot where the sole had come loose and he stood for a moment, shaking his foot. Since he could hear neither the birdsong, nor the hum of insects, nor the trickle of water in the ditch it wasn't surprising that he also did not hear a distant rumble. He reached down to loosen the laces and then lifted the boot up to shake out the offending stone, when the unheard train knocked him sideways and ran over his legs just below the knee. The boot in his hand flew up in an arc that carried it some distance from the track. The boot on his other foot, made it into the ambulance with him where despite the best efforts of the crew his heart finally stopped.

Forbidden Fruit

Dawn Morgan

The sound of the pealing bells blew in and out on the breeze as Matthew walked towards the church. The village reeked with prettiness, every thatched roof snipped neatly, the leaded windows twinkling in the June sunshine as if flirting with him, and all the cottage walls painted pastel shades that were as sickly as the cupcakes in the tea room.

The sight of Pink Lady apples arranged in a pyramid outside the grocer's shop reminded him that he was thirsty after his three hour drive, and their neat arrangement irritated him. It was like everything else in this village, stage-managed to appear perfect. He stopped to choose one, picking a plump fruit with glossy skin that looked bursting with life, leaving a hole in the neat display.

Inside the shop, the grocer looked at the single apple with distaste.

'We sell them by the kilo,' he said.

'How much is a kilo?' asked Matthew, taking out his wallet and removing a bank card.

'£3.50, but we only take cards if it's over five pounds.'

Matthew gave the man a level stare and replaced his card. Fishing in his pocket, he removed a handful of coins and counted out four pounds, which he pushed across the counter.

'Keep the change,' he said, picking up his apple and tossing it into the air, catching it again with a snatch before turning to leave the shop.

'Don't you want your other apples?' called the grocer.

'No, just the one,' said Matthew, from the doorway.

He bit noisily into the fruit when he reached the street, a sense of satisfaction as the skin was parted by his teeth, the liquid of it sweet on his tongue and lips. The grocer stared after him with a kind of greed. Not for the apple, but for knowledge. Who was this new customer, where did he come from, and why did he pay £4 for an apple?

Matthew continued on his way, wiping juice from his chin, glancing up at the bright sky with its cauliflower clouds. It was a perfect summer Saturday, ideal for a wedding. The sweetness of the church bells increased as he got closer, their notes tripping over one another like a tune on a child's tongue.

Then they stopped. Matthew stopped with them. Leaning one shoulder against a dusky pink wall, he watched the bride emerge from a Mercedes, lace rising around her, billowing in the wind, so that she walked to the church with one hand on her father's arm and the other pushing down the fabric of her three thousand pound dress.

Matthew grinned, finished his apple in two large bites and threw the core over the church wall to seed itself by a leaning headstone. Then he folded his arms and waited until the church door was pulled shut and all sounds of the wedding service were cut off. With a nod, he straightened, brushed rosy dust from his dark blue shirt and glanced at his watch. He decided to give it fifteen minutes and spent the time strolling around the churchyard, reading birth and death dates, the sadness of orphans, widowers lamenting the passing of the girls they had loved.

He was scowling again before he went to the church door with his hands in his pockets, head bent forward as if he intended to batter his way in with his crown. The last time he'd been inside a church was that day, that Saturday, when the organist had played for forty minutes looking over his shoulder while Matthew waited at the head of the aisle, hands folded in front of him, his best man putting his hand to his pocket over and over again, feeling for the ring. The noise of people whispering grew so loud that when the organist gave up, Matthew could hear actual words.

He paused now, drew a breath through his nose, turned the iron ring and pushed, misjudging the pressure he would need against the well-oiled hinges and striding into the church with a splash of sunshine that turned every head in the pews towards him.

'This at last is bone of my bones and flesh of my

flesh,' the bridegroom was saying, reading from a slip of paper held low in his hand. He looked up at the disturbance and Matthew held up a hand of apology before closing the church door and standing against the rear wall. There was some throat clearing among the congregation. The bride turned her beautiful head and peered at him through the dim light.

'Please, go on,' said Matthew, his voice resonant in the cool air of the church, and edged with his military crispness, which caused a ripple of appreciation among the bridesmaids.

The bride visibly flinched at his voice, and Matthew felt a warmth in his veins as he watched the petals of her bouquet trembling. The rector leaned forward to speak to the couple in an urgent hiss. With a shake of her head, Eve turned to the fresh-faced groom again and nodded at him to continue. But she looked sideways at Matthew while the boy spoke.

'She shall be called Woman, because she was taken out of Man,' said the groom, mumbling and holding his paper at the level of his bride's breasts.

Mathew had clearly missed the part of the service where the rector asked if anyone knew of a reason why the two could not be married. But he wouldn't have spoken at that moment. Too trite. He continued to watch and listen as the boy finished his reading. There was a pause while Eve took out her own slip of paper, which had been tucked into her bouquet. As she began to speak, Matthew fed on the sight of her, the long pale neck and fine brow, naturally fair hair scraped back under a ring of lilies, a delicious expanse of bare shoulder glowing above her sleeveless dress.

'Therefore, a man shall leave his father and his mother and hold fast to his wife,' she said, her voice wavering and falling to the flagstones like leaves. 'And they shall become one flesh.'

This would be the moment, if Matthew was going to act, before the couple spoke their legal vows and exchanged rings. But he waited and watched, his brow knitting as Eve's voice shivered prettily through the church, and finally she held out her white hand towards the groom, her eyes still flitting towards Matthew.

There were still a few seconds when Matthew could march to the front of the church, gain the gathering's full attention, and describe the beast that he had made with Eve's back, less than a week before, the skin between her shoulder blades running with sweat. The perfect revenge. More perfect, even, than the seduction itself, which he had managed as slickly as any other night manoeuvre.

But did he really want all the trouble? Fathers shaking fists, balls of spittle in the corners of their mouths; mothers holding hands up to their loose, powdered throats? And then what would he do? Carry her off? He'd no doubt she'd go with him, given a second chance. Even as she stood with her fingers spread towards the boy, she was glancing at Matthew under her curled lashes. But now that he had come to it, the thought of Eve's perspiring back against the leather of his Saab seemed faintly repulsive, and he found that his intent was draining away, like the colour from the bride's cheeks.

With a twist of his lips, he left the church as quickly as he had entered, the rector's voice following him into the sunlight. Pausing on the broad steps, he savoured a sense of completion that gave him almost as much satisfaction as the girl had done. But as the heat hit him, after the chill of the church, he felt the beginnings of thirst, then hunger, and he thought that perhaps he would have more fruit after all. Feeling the weight of coins in his pocket, he set off to buy another apple, leaving the door of the church gaping open behind him.

Keep the Home Fires Burning

Dawn Wyndham

Pity I was too frail and old to go to the ceremony. I'd had a special invitation too. They wanted me there, me being an almost-witness of that day. And, after all, my granddaughter Hélène was the Maire's secretary. She'd helped with the organisation and said it was important to her for me to be there, but even the short car journey was too much for me and my old legs wouldn't have let me stand for long, so I watched it on the television. It seemed strange seeing Oradour on the News. During the occupation I used to go there every day on the tram, working as receptionist and general help at the Hotel Avril, just by the church. It was a peaceful place then. Apart from the shortages the war had mostly passed us by. We never saw a soldier, let alone a German one.

It was broadcast live. The President of Germany, Joachim Gauck, was visiting Oradour Sur Glane after sixty-nine years. The only German leader ever to visit the village, still like an open wound, preserved exactly as it was after that day; what was left of it. The first one to confront what his countrymen had done on that sunny June Saturday in 1944. About time, but they should have dropped a bomb on the place, wiped the awful evidence from the face of the planet.

My daughter and great grandchildren wanted to stay behind with me to share the occasion's significance, but I wanted to be on my own, alone with my past. It's not the same for them, for the youngsters. 'Move on,' they say, 'it's a different world now…' So, they sat me in my favourite chair with a flask of coffee and a plate of macarons beside me, bright green, pink and chocolate brown, and left without me. In memory of that day I'd put on the blue-grey dress that Bertrand had loved me to wear, kept safe all these years. Too big now over my thin old bones and a bit smelly: must have been the moth-balls.

On the screen the village looks too clinical to disturb me, for the moment at least. My first impression - and this is embarrassing to admit - is of some elaborate, deserted film set. It's unnaturally clean; an empty road, overhung by lush trees, a pair of tram-rails snaking towards buildings. There are no sounds, no sign of any kind of life.

I remember what it's like to stand on that ruined street, next to a sign that begged 'SILENCE'. Masonry and metal make a face of the past; the roofless houses are jagged teeth, windows sightless eyes in stone skulls. In every house there is still something left after the looting and burning: iron bedsteads, Singer sewing machines, bicycles, wine racks, pumps, various machines, cars burnt in their garages. In the burned out church the bell lies where it fell from the tower, tortured by fire into a huge, deformed lump, its tongue welded into its throat. In places you see nature's touching attempts to conceal the tormented truth: ivy creeps over the ruins. Man-made evidence of the present mocks the past; incongruous scaffolding supporting a dangerous wall here, re-pointed stonework there.

I poured myself a cup of coffee and knocked the macarons to the floor as I took one. Ça alors! I love macarons. I'd have eaten the lot but I couldn't bend enough to pick them up from where they'd rolled.

I remember the day it happened. Every detail. The baby had been screaming all night. 'Evèe, Evèe, Evèe, what's wrong?' I sang. Her beetroot-red face screwed up, eyes shut tight, tears seeping from the corners. Tiny fists clenched and punching the air as she wailed, legs bent and kicking, the noise stopping only for a brief, heart-rending, sobbing sigh. I was bone-achingly tired. This was the third night I had carried her downstairs to the kitchen, leaving Bertrand to sleep so he would be fit to work in Hubert Desourteaux's garage just down the road from Avril's. They were busy: There was a big demand for modifying cars to run on coal to get round the petrol shortage. I rocked Evèe wearily. Teething. That would be it, poor scrap.

That Saturday morning was a work day, a school day, so I asked Maman to take care of her while I went to work. I usually took her with me and she sat happily in her pushchair, watching proceedings and responding with a gurgle to the occasional attention from customers. Today I was glad of the respite. I queued for the tram in a trance, the lack of sleep edging my concentration down a tunnel. I sat at the very back, in the far corner. The sound and movement of the tram on that warm June day were a lullaby. I fell asleep.

'Madame!' The voice was urgent. 'Madame, wake up! We have arrived at the terminus.'

'Where are we?' I blinked at the tram driver.

'Limoges, Madame. We are in Limoges'

'Limoges! What time is it? '

'It's three thirty Madame'

'Oh no!' I said. 'I'm so late for work. I should have got off at Oradour. What time is the next tram back?'

'We're not sure. There seems to be a problem with the line. We're sending a test tram with just a driver and an engineer. If that gets back alright there will be another one leaving at just before six.'

Well, I was stuck. It was the tram or nothing. It would be hours, but I had to wait. I didn't know then what was happening in Oradour. I didn't know then that I would never see Bertrand again. Or anyone I had ever known there again.

The soldiers of the Waffen SS had come, and herded the people together. The men had been taken to garages and barns, the women and small children led down the main road and driven into the church. From there, they'd heard the firing of the machine guns as our men were shot; then the noise of the children being collected from the schools, the sound of their wooden shoes mingled with the heavy tramp of soldiers' boots like the beat of an awful drum. They'd encouraged the children to sing as they marched them down to join the others in the house of God.

The incendiary device they'd placed on the altar hadn't detonated properly, so the thick smoke they hoped would choke the women, children and babies imprisoned there just sharpened their fear and panic. They'd had to resort to hand grenades and machine guns through the windows and, finally, fire to finish the job. 246 women and 207 children died in the church carnage. They threw straw and petrol on the men too, some still alive. Everything was burned, every building, every home, every veteran and every baby. Hearts stopped, watches stopped; brains and glasses melted. 642 had been murdered in a matter of hours. Afterwards only 52 were identifiable. Just nine were women and three were children.

I shifted in my seat and shivered, even though the September day was sunny and warm. That macaron wasn't sitting well. I had indigestion. I rubbed my chest, hoping to burp.

The TV cameras zoomed in. Joachim Gauck was a white-haired, upright man. He was escorted by our own President, François Hollande. They walked in silence up the main street, past the sign that every visitor passes at the entrance to the village: 'Souviens-toi.' Remember. They say he has been called Germany's answer to Nelson Mandela, as a man who had been closely watched by the hated Stasi secret police in communist East Germany. After the wall fell he was put in charge of all their files and exposing their crimes in the name of justice and reconciliation. Pah! The irony of it made me smile to myself as I watched. Gauck was Germany here, far from the Fatherland, but still its son, next to Hollande, the strutting France of war-time masculinity, from cropped women to the Liberation. They held hands. They held hands! To symbolise the reconciliation between France and Germany, they were saying.

Then there was a glimpse of the onlookers. There was my Evelyn and her daughter Hélène, next to Hélène's sister Sylvie and Sylvie's twins Albert and Jean. My heart lurched, (doing my indigestion no good at all.) Generations of my family standing in that haunted place. I should be one of those ghosts. I shouldn't have had these years of past. They should have been denied their future. We should all be ghosts, either dead or unborn.

By seven o'clock that day I was on the tram back from Limoges. The village was still burning when it stopped on the bridge at Oradour. The soldiers got on and checked all our papers. About twenty of us, those of us from Oradour or nearby – including me, from Bussiere Poitevine – were made to get off before they waved the tram on its way, turned back to Limoges. I gagged on the smoke. The stench was indescribable; burned human flesh and petrol, gunpowder and terror. Where was Bertrand?

They marched us round the burning village, past untold horror, to a field. We could see the soldiers setting fire to more houses, throwing grenades into them. Noise and smoke and mayhem. I held the hand of a child, Cecile, she said her name was, her mother holding the other, my bowels turning to liquid with fear. As we stood on the grass they went into a huddle. Voices rose in a heated discussion while we stood in mute terror, not understanding anything they were saying. So this was it. We were going to be shot.

What looked like a senior officer walked towards us. He had a bicycle. Why? I'll never know, but he handed it to me and shouted, 'Run!' The knife-edge of mercy and murder had tilted towards life. They let us all go.

I should have perished with the others. Perhaps I was wrong when I said I remember every detail. I barely remember cycling home. I know I was sobbing, shaking, hardly able to pedal, grief-stricken and trembling. The strangest thing kept going through my mind. The dogs. I could not shake off the image of the village's dogs. Their piteous crying, tails clamped firmly between their legs as they faithfully rummaged and sniffed through the ruins in anguish, trying to find the owners they had loved.

Music. A commercial break: Sunny smiles advertising toothpaste and cars.

They resumed the news report in the church. I

turned uncomfortably in my chair to look at a face that has claimed me all these years because he has always looked so much like Bertrand. Robert Hebras, one of the two remaining living survivors, is standing between the two leaders. I knew him well. He was Bertrand's closest friend back then. He was younger than me, just nineteen at the time. Wounded, he hid under the corpses of others who were machine-gunned. He lost his mother and two sisters, Georgette and little Denise, just nine years old.

They are in front of that altar, next to a burned and flattened pushchair - so like Evée's - left in place where it had been found. They have their arms around him, supporting him. 'I was consumed by hatred and vengeance for a long time,' he said. 'Any earlier would have been too soon, but now we must be reconciled with the Germans.'

I want to pick up a rock and hurl it at the television! My pulse raced with fury. I started shivering. I was so cold. Damned pain in my chest was worse! Fighting for breath I hauled myself out of the chair and stumbled to the cupboard. I pulled out Bertrand's old jacket, kept where he had always hung it. So long since I had last touched it, smelled it. His. It still held him in its fabric. I wrapped the bigness of it around my shoulders, feeling it engulf me and lay myself down with him, sinking to the floor.

Just out of reach, I could see a pink macaron under my chair.

Only Time Will Tell

Sue Wright

There were three men in the agreement. They made an unlikely group, sitting in the sunshine, each with a beer. Tom was shading his eyes against the sun, Dick was stroking his beard in a contemplative manner and Harry was cupping his ear in order to focus on the conversation rather than the voices at the next table. Each of them drew his glass towards his chest, in absent-minded choreography. One fat and two thin faces stared into the distance until the fat man finally reneged on their self-induced silence.

'Down the hatch.'

'Right you are.'

'Iechyd da.'

All three stood up, slid their glasses to clink together in the centre of the table, nodded and walked away.

The agreement weighed heaviest on Tom. Perhaps because the weight of it was heavier in his greater bulk or maybe it was his sensitive temperament. Nevertheless, it was a terrible burden for him and the strain of it eventually carried him off. He had been bending down to take off his shoes and socks one hot

Sunday afternoon when, losing his balance, he keeled over. His heart had finally given up on keeping him upright, or even alive, and as he slumped to the floor his last words had lurched out of his mouth, halfway between an exclamation and a grunt. Since there were no witnesses, his final contribution to the world went unheard.

Had Dick and Harry known, they might have come to the funeral, but then again, they might not. Dick was living rough, while Harry was making his way on foot from John O'Groats to Land's End. So far he had reached Leeds but it had already taken him two years. He sometimes thought about the secret as his feet trundled on. It troubled him a great deal that he didn't know whether the others were still committed to their pact. At other times, for mile after mile he didn't think about anything at all. By the time he reached his destination, he'd been walking for so long that he'd almost forgotten how to keep still. He was so used to driving himself forward that he took to the open road again after a rest of only a week or so. Another month and he arrived back at his own starting point, where he and his two companions had drunk beer together years before.

The pub was still there, derelict now with boarded windows, but he walked round the back and clambered over a fence into the garden. A broken chair by the back door slid sideways as he approached. He kicked it out of the way and seeing that both the lock and handle had been smashed, he pushed the door inwards. A scuffling sound made him turn and peer into the darkest corner, a heap of clothes confronted him. He poked it with his foot as his eyes became accustomed to the dark and was startled when a sallow face turned to look at him. He took a step back.

'Oh my god, it's you!'

'So it is, so it is.'

Dick stood up, a ragged scarecrow of a man, his beard traced with cobwebs and his hands holding onto a book.

'Well?'

'Well what?'

'Is the secret still intact?'

'You tell me.'

'My lips are as sealed as ever.'

'Me too. What about Tom?'

'I saw in the paper that he'd gone.'

'Gone where?'

'Dead.'

'Oh. Just us then.'

He looked across at the book meaningfully and Dick slid the volume into his coat pocket and folded his arms.

'What's that?'

'Nothing you need to see.'

'Don't tell me you've written it down.'

'It's all right, it's written in code.'

'Fool.'

Harry lunged forward and Dick leaned back. In the ensuing scuffle, Harry got the better of him, being fitter by far. Being pushed suddenly backwards, Dick lost his footing and fell to the ground. Harry reached for the book but failed to grasp it. Dick stood up again and threw the book over the bar and headed for the door. Harry barred his way out.

'Why?'

'Why what?'

'Why did you write it down?'

'It was driving me insane. It kept trying to get out of me. I thought that if I wrote it down, it would be satisfied and leave me alone. I'd never have to think of it ever again. I've had enough of it. It has already killed one of us and I was going to be next. And you, what about you? Why all this walking and walking. Perhaps you're trying to get it out of your system too.'

'Maybe.'

'All this time wasted, trying to hold it in. Why don't we just shout it from the rooftops and be done with it and then we can all relax and get on with life.'

'You're not serious?'

'What if I am?'

Both men stood in silence as they walked together out into the sunshine once more. Both heads turned as the church clock struck the hour.

'It's time.'

'Ah, so it is, so it is.'

For Mercy's Sake

Sal Starling

She stared at the bed. How had her mother kept this a secret?

The first bundle she'd found was at the bottom of a drawer of old photographs; a thousand pounds in ten-pound notes. Faith spent the next hour searching through the cupboards and drawers of her mother's bedroom, finding more bundles hidden under clothes and at the back of wardrobes. She laid the cash across the stripped bed and sat beside it; twelve thousand pounds, but where had it come from? Faith always collected her mother's pension and care allowance herself and knew that every penny went on shopping, rent and bills. They didn't go short, but neither did they buy anything they didn't need. She also knew that her parents had never trusted banks; they were old school, never borrowed money and always paid bills with cash. No banks, debt or savings. At least that's what she thought, until now.

She sifted once more through the notes' rose-tinted images of William Shakespeare and Florence Nightingale. Was old currency still legal tender? A quick search revealed that withdrawn notes could still be deposited at a bank. She tipped the photographs into a carrier bag, placed the money into a holdall, and sat awhile.

Faith packed a few of her personal belongings alongside the money and visited each room in the house. She switched off lights, pulled out plugs and checked that windows were shut. She pulled the front door closed behind her and paused for a moment to touch its peeling red paint - conjuring an image of her and her father painting it so many years ago when she was a child. Faith smiled at the memory of her Dad's face, spattered with red paint which took days to wash off and made him look like he had some terrible disease. She slipped the key into her purse and walked away.

Regency Hill was steep, and the walk from the bus stop became tiring as Faith hauled the holdall and carrier bag of memories towards her sister's house at the top. She rang the bell and waited in the Georgian-style porch. Faith and her mother never saw much of Helen as she was a very busy housewife with two children, a successful husband and a beautiful home. Faith rang the bell again and waited patiently.

Helen had been nineteen and just starting her degree when their mother first became ill. It made sense for young Faith to give up work to look after her. She had always been the less ambitious daughter, and Faith graciously felt that her job as a trainee librarian was less important than her sister's dream of becoming a barrister.

While Helen made coffee, Faith sat on the edge of the white Italian sofa and slid the photographs onto the marble coffee table.

'The funeral went well,' said Helen, passing Faith a tiny espresso with one hand, a large whisky in the other. 'What will you do now - without Mum to look after?'

Faith had no idea what she'd do. She was lost. For twelve years her every waking hour had been spent caring for their mother, seeing she was fed, clean and comfortable in between changing beds, washing and doing the housework. Respite came each Friday afternoon in the shape of a Marie Curie nurse when, for just a few hours, Faith was able to visit the library and immerse herself in romantic worlds where everyone lived happily ever after.

'I found these and thought you might like them,' said Faith.

Helen sat beside her and spread the photographs across the table. Immaculate nails flicked through them until she picked out a photo of two schoolchildren standing in the grounds of a grand Edwardian building.

'I didn't know Mum had this; I must have sent it with her Christmas card a couple of years ago.'

'How are the kids?' asked Faith.

'They're fine; Martha loves St Benedict's. In fact, we have a problem in the holidays because she'd rather stay with her friends in the dorm than come with us to Antigua – can you believe that?' Helen forced a smile. 'Poor George's finding it rather tough though. He doesn't like sharing a room with the big boys. Geoffrey says it will make a man of him, but I think eight is too young to be away so much ... don't you?'

Faith shrugged and looked away - feeling that further discussion may prompt Helen's tears.

'This is a nice picture of you,' said Faith, holding up a wedding photo.

'Yes ... I was happy back then.'

'Back then?'

Helen gave a full smile with empty eyes, 'Oh, you know - things change. Geoffrey works such long hours lately, can get a bit lonely at times. Perhaps I should go back to work? Still, I don't take anything for granted - we wouldn't have all this without him putting in the hours.' Helen swept her arm across the opulent room and went to refill her glass. 'Damn migraine,' she said, slumping on the sofa with a pack of painkillers. Faith watched her knock back the tablets with a large swig of whisky.

It wasn't how Mum used to take them, she thought; it always took her several attempts to swallow just one morphine capsule. Sometimes, Faith would open the capsule and mix the contents with a spoonful of warm tea, making it easier to swallow. Second capsules were sometimes hidden away in the little ballerina jewellery box under her bed.

'Look Faith - remember this?' Helen held up a monochrome picture. 'It was our last family holiday before Dad died ... remember? I was sixteen and you were ... oh ... you were in love!' Helen smiled at the thought of her sister being in love for the first and, as it turned out, the last time. 'What was his name? ... Steve!'

'David. His name was David,' whispered Faith, slipping the photograph into her pocket. 'I might go away for a while,' she said.

'Go away? You never go anywhere. What will you do on your own? Why don't you stay in Mum's house? We could spend more time together, I'd like that,' said Helen.

'I think it's time I moved on.' Faith was beginning to believe her own words. There was nothing here for her now.

She pulled on her coat and thought back to the day her mother died, of how she had helped her with the contents of the little ballerina box. Her last act of love. No-one knew what she had done and it was to remain that way - between her, her mother and her conscience. She needed time; time to get away, to think, to come to terms with her loss, and to try and escape the guilt which weighed heavier than the holdall she picked up in the hallway.

Helen followed her to the door, 'Let me give you some money. I won't need it back.' Faith shook her head.

'I'm okay, I have money ... savings.'

It crossed her mind to tell her sister about the money; but why? Twelve thousand would be a drop in the ocean to Helen. It was a fortune to Faith. It was her future.

Helen stood in the porch, wrapped her cashmere cardigan across her chest, and watched her sister walk down the hill and out of sight.

'Just one way, please.'

Faith stroked a thumb across the train ticket, the first she'd seen since the family holiday in Weston fifteen years ago. It had been a nice place, with happy memories. As good a place as any, she thought, to start over.

A train groaned slowly in to the station and, as the doors hissed open, Faith stuffed the ticket into her pocket, tightened the belt of her coat, and picked up the bag full of money and hope.

Birds of a Feather

Dawn Wyndham

Padding down the stairs to start the day, the narrow strip of ceramic tiles that border the rug was cold beneath her bare feet. She heard a 'Click'. Good, the coffee machine had turned itself on with the timer. The windows creaked as she opened them, the escaping smell of coffee skimming past her nostrils. When she had put the pan on and bread in the toaster to make breakfast, she was drawn back to the window.

There was mist in the hollow of the valley, like water in the bowl of righteous hands cupped to receive the day's blessing. The overnight storm had left clouds marooned high on the tops of the hills and the air was cold and still, as clean as if it had never been breathed by any living thing. She sighed, filling her lungs to the brim, surprised to see her breath take shape, a cobweb of air that only a second before had been warm inside her. She breathed out through her mouth a few more times, watching her breath fade away into the garden. Then she closed the window, sipping the mug of coffee that had waited on the window ledge, relinquishing its heat to the morning air.

The smell of porridge catching to the pan mingled with the smoke rising from the toaster. Anna looked at the clock. Lord! Late again! She was cross with herself for daydreaming and now the breakfast was burning too! She tutted at herself as she stirred the pan.

'Morning,' he said as he hurried in, shirt half on, half off. She regarded his back, muscular and smooth, looking at the scratches he'd got from the thorn bush he'd fallen heavily into yesterday. He strolled languidly towards her. His tall athletic frame had a subtle air of menace, of danger, of unstrung animal energy.

'You'll be late.'

'No, I won't,' he said, grinning. 'I'm going straight to site today, so I've got half an hour leeway.'

She flew a glance at him, smiled and relaxed.

'I'll make the porridge again then?'

'Nah, I like it burned.'

He gave her a peck on the cheek before he sat and buttered the blackened toast. She regarded the bruises and grazes on his back.

'I'll get some Arnica ointment. That looks like it could turn nasty.'

He shifted his weight to look over his shoulder, trying to see his own back.

'It's going to be fine. I've had worse.' He saluted her, a sharp comic military-style gesture. 'It's only a scratch, Ma'am.'

She smiled back at him, reassured, thinking how nearly perfect their lives had become since they'd moved here. To this house, in a remote village by the sea - after he was offered the post as a Marine Biologist in the state university. It could have been made for him, giving him freedom from regular hours by being an independent researcher. It left him time to pursue the obligations of his birth right.

It was a great place for Anna too. The area's local traditions of quilting and craftwork were world renowned and so her work sold well. She had picked up the particular style of the local artisans easily, adding her own spin, acquired at her grandmother Bushka's knee. The quilts and wall hangings she created in her workshop at the end of the garden sold well and made a satisfying income.

Breakfast finished, he pulled the long-sleeved polo shirt over his head and grabbed his parka. A feather floated to the ground behind his back.

'Okay. That's me. I'm off.'

She stood to hug him as he left.

'See you later.'

They'd lived in the big double-gabled Manse for almost twelve of the 130 years it had stood here. Perched on top of a hill, overlooking the little hamlet and the chapel, it sat like a handsome squatting guardian of the breath-taking view. Pausing at the big window, she looked up at the horizon. The hackles on the back of her neck rose and shivered as she saw the sky from her earthbound view.

Birds of a Feather

Every year in late February there was a run of days when she could definitely say the light was back. That some milestone had been reached and the light spilled into the world from a sun suddenly higher in the sky. Two birds circled overhead, chevrons mewing loudly across the valley, silhouetted against clouds of a myriad monochrome shades. She sent them a thought of greeting. The cold wind lifted the grasses and moved the thin shoots of the leafless shrubs so the sun shone through them. The light was razor sharp, edging branches and twigs of the willow and apple trees so the garden was all slanting stripes of light and shade. Too soft to be called a sparkle, but the light was giving the world a spring clean. On the skyline the upturned limbs of winter trees stretched black against the light. She could hear them giving their own salute to the sun.

She hummed to herself as she made her way to her workshop, skirting the hem of the woodland that was the rear boundary to their land. It was cold. She wore a blue pom-pom hat over her auburn hair and a thick coat she would take off once the art room had warmed up. She was not quite beautiful. Her eyes were too far apart, her neck too long, her mouth too wide, but added together she had a charismatic sensuality. Although not tall, she had legs that appeared to start at her shoulder-blades and she walked with immense ease and poise, incapable of a graceless movement.

Approaching the door, Anna thought how the

structure had matured and been added to over the years as her business had grown. The round window and stained glass of the small art room were junk-shop buys when they couldn't afford anything else. Now, as the ante-room to the bigger structure behind, the character they lent to the otherwise modern unit gave a satisfying sense of permanence.

She knelt to put kindling and logs in the small pot-bellied wood burner. She lowered her eyes, remembering the intimate touch when they had kissed, the apple smell of his hair, the skin-to-skin scrape of cheek against beard. The heat of his hands on her shoulders as he pulled her closer, the familiar tightening in her pelvis like a primitive call as her desire quickened.

'Heey. Come on Anna,' she admonished herself. 'Get some bloody work done.'

Hanging over the smaller pieces of commercial work, mostly commissions, was a huge collage. An elaborate mix of tapestry, painting, applique and embroidered beadwork, it strung the length of her workshop yards long, covering that side of the walls. It was her personal masterpiece, made of years of care and loving toil - a physical manifestation of her and Henry. Of their heritage. It perfectly told their story.

It was a busy day. Anna was absorbed in her work, head down, concentrating hard, with the characteristic chewing of her lower lip that she didn't know she was doing until she stopped. Around lunch time she was disturbed by a delivery of chiffons and embroidery silks she had been waiting for so she decided it was time for a break.

She had a small gas ring in the studio, a legacy from camping trips in the Highlands before they had their VW camper van with a fully functioning hob. She lit it and put the small whistling kettle on it. Turning to get a cup, she looked out of the window and could see her neighbour's dog limping across the lawn. It was unusual for him to be loose and he looked distressed and injured. She rushed out to him, taking a length of cloth from the bench to use as a leash to capture him.

'Here, boy.'

She approached him calmly, holding out a biscuit she'd grabbed from the caddy as an afterthought on her way out.

'There, it's okay.'

She kept her voice low and soft. His paw was bleeding and he was carrying his leg. He limped over to her – or rather to the biscuit in her hand and she put her arm around him as she deftly looped the string of cloth through his collar. He was trembling.

Just then a head popped up over the hedge. It was Ken Harris, who lived next door.

'Oh! Buddy! There you are!' The relief and concern in his voice was palpable.

'I'll be right there. I'll have to go round the front. I'm so glad you caught him. Is he okay? He got out and a delivery van didn't see him. It was reversing out of your drive, so thankfully it was going very slowly, but it did hit him and he's only small. Please say he's okay.'

Anna tried to play down her concern.

'He seems alright, but his paw is bleeding and his leg is clearly hurting him. I'll bring him to the front.'

Buddy was a black and white Jack Russell, small enough to be scooped up in Anna's arms. She could feel his heart fluttering against her chest as he surrendered to her cuddle.

The door, left open, was swinging in the breeze that wafted into the studio, adding to the moving air like a fan, riffling the organza and ribbons left at the edge of the workbench. The kettle had boiled dry and the plastic handle was starting to melt and burn. Suddenly the smoke burst to flame, licking at the waving ribbons.

Anna's special animal senses gave her an empathy with Buddy that was total and comforting. He lifted his head and licked her chin, grateful for her closeness. She could feel his fear and sent him thoughts of calm and reassurance.

'You're going to be fine,' she breathed into his fur. When she had made her way up the path and got to the drive at the front of her house Mr. Harris was already hurrying towards them.

'Oh! Buddy!' He reached for him and the dog struggled slightly in Anna's hold, eager to be reunited with his master, his tail already twitching to a wag.

'I'll take him straight to the vet to get checked over. Looks like that paw could do with a stitch or two and he'll need to be x-rayed.' Mr. Harris had come prepared with a small crocheted blanket, clearly out of Buddy's bed.

'Thank you Anna. Thank you so much. I'll let you know how we get on, but I can't thank you enough.' As she handed the wagging dog over she knew he was going to be fine and she could feel his pain was already subsiding.

She watched as her elderly neighbour put the dog in the back of his car and drove off.

She first saw the smoke as she turned the corner of the house. Her heart leapt. Running as fast as she could she crashed through the workshop door. The ribbons and fabric on the bench were well alight, but worse – the front edge of her tapestry was on fire! The stitching and artistry were already ash along the lower edge for about three feet, the flames climbing slowly to consume higher up her precious fable. Coughing from the smoke she made a dash for the fire extinguisher kept by the wood stove in the back of the ante-room. Henry had insisted on it although she had felt it was over-cautious. Thank heaven it was there.

With a speed born of panic she activated the canister. In seconds the fire was drenched with CO_2.

She stood there, sobbing.

'Hello?' Henry was surprised to hear her voice. She rarely called him during the work day so he knew something must be wrong.

'Henry....' She stifled her sobs.

'What on earth has happened?' Henry asked, alarmed and worried.

She told him the sequence of her day; the dog, the fire, the devastating damage to her masterpiece.

'Are you sure it's out? I'll be right there. I'm about an hour away, but I'll get there as quickly as I can.'

She nodded.

'Anna?'

She realized he couldn't see a nod.

'Drive safely Henry. See you soon.'

'Yes, make yourself a cup of tea or pour yourself a drink and stay out of the workshop until I get there, okay?'

'Yes.'

She hung up and headed for the kitchen.

They stood in the studio, surveying the damage. Henry had his arm around her shoulder. She leaned into his solidity.

He squeezed her shoulder.

'It could have been a lot worse.'

They had swept up most of the damaged cloth and paraphernalia and she could see the real extent of the fire clearly. The bench was scorched and she had lost some materials, but it was the tapestry that was most badly damaged.

'Oh Henry! It's not completely ruined, but it will take a lot of work.'

'But it's not lost. You can still repair it.' He regarded the cinders. 'It's still mostly intact and the legend lives in our hearts, in our blood. It is us.'

Even so damaged it was an impressive work of art. It told the story of the beginning of Anna and Henry's time, when people and animals lived together on earth and there was no difference between them. Ape, human, tiger, swan, even tree and water, all had spirit. All had soul. It was an illustration of when all creatures touched and talked easily, were together as naturally as breathing and warm as sunlight.

When communication held a magic.

When a random word spoken in chance, a wish or a whisper, held a power that could shape the world and cast a spell so compelling it would be handed down through the generations; the same compulsion that was there in them both. An ancient inherited genetic mutation which allowed them to voluntarily invoke a change. Untie themselves. Unfold from human reality into a truth long forgotten by men. To become other beings. It was their exclusive shared joy. But to do it independently would break the genetic code that binds them and risk losing the gift, the talent.

With the privilege came peril. She thought of the times when they had been in mortal danger, the most recent the crash to the ground that had caused the grazes and bruises on Henry's back. Just as the call to change compelled them, gave them the irresistible impetus to morph their human form, an unexpected hazard, a glitch in the fabric of time, an age-old oath spoken aloud and long forgotten could disturb the magic and jeopardise them both. The chimera of existence rippled softly in their shared world.

He lifted her chin so she was looking at him.

'Come on, let's go.'

Hand in hand they turned and walked out of the workshop onto the path, where the sun had been waiting for them.

She was squinting upward, her hand above her brow, but still she couldn't make out enough for an identification. Far above, wheeling on the thermals was a bird of prey, perhaps a kite. No, a buzzard. She could feel him up there, but was it him? Should she go now, before she got the call? She almost laughed to herself. From so high in the sky Henry could see the detail of the buttons on her shirt, but, even trying hard, she couldn't tell what species he was.

Then it came, surging through her. The undeniable tug. The call to transform, to unfurl, uncurl as string is unknotted, as seaweed swells when returned to the sea, to the element where it belongs. His appeal did not go unanswered.

Flying a metaphysical trapeze, she swung into the transformation and, like changing channels, she suddenly found herself in another time and place.

Joining him, they were both birds in the sky, surfing gravity. Their speckled brown and white bodies soared across the sunset. They answered the other's call loudly, proudly. The silver linings of the clouds were sliced by outspread, beautiful wings. Their figures stood prominent in the bright light above, with only small pockets of cloud to hide them. Silhouettes against the orange-kissed heavens, they danced.

Only an hour ago they would have been pale against a blue sky, but the twilight was advancing and soon they would be lost in blackness, roosting side by side with head tucked under wing until dawn.

It Never Rains, But it Pours

Dawn Morgan

Daniel says he loves our warm, sudden weather that clatters on the palm leaves and makes craters in the dust.

'Very different from our British drizzle,' he said, the first time I served him in the bar. 'That's glum stuff. Even the sheep get depressed.'

The idea of hillsides filled with sad sheep made me laugh, although I've only seen sheep in books.

'You're a little early for the monsoon,' I told him. 'The rains don't start properly until next month.'

'Oh, I like the build-up, your daily deluge at five o'clock,' he said with a smile. 'And this is the perfect way to enjoy it.'

He raised his glass to me and went to sit in a chair, watching the storm boil in the sky, leaning forward to gaze at the rain through the open French doors. As I served the other customers, I noticed that he sat perfectly still while the rain churned on the pathways and made an orange-peel surface on the swimming pool. After the noise and wetness had subsided, and the slow tick of the ceiling fans could be heard again, he drained his glass and nodded to me as he went out for the evening. When he came back it was very late and there were no other customers in the bar. He sat and talked to me.

'Call me Daniel,' he said, smiling into my eyes with a frankness that would have seemed rude from any other guest.

But there was something innocent about Daniel's face which meant that he never caused offence. Over the following week, I often saw him talking to other guests, who looked alarmed at first, but were soon chatting with him eagerly. He even approached the tall American woman who has been staying at the hotel alone. I put plenty of ice in her glass and only a little gin. It's well known that alcohol is dehydrating in this heat, especially for women.

One evening when the bar was empty again, Daniel asked me what he should see on the island before he left. He gave me a slanted smile as he spoke, as if my answer would be a secret between us. I told him he should see the greenness of the island, away from the beach with its roar of jet skis and trails of spilt fuel. He should go up into the hills where you can't hear the whine of traffic from the coast road, or smell its greasy vapour.

I also told him to avoid the tourist places, like the pink beach with its hardened little monkeys who will steal anything, even a wallet. He laughed loudly at that, leaning his head back, and asked if the animals took their cash into the city for a spending spree, or just frittered it away in the bars. I laughed too, feeling the rush of it like liquid. Together, while he rested his folded arms on the bar and leaned towards me, we imagined all the things that the monkeys would buy.

When I told him about my grandmother, who remembers the island as it used to be, he wanted to meet her. So, on my day off, he drove us up into the mountains, the three of us. My grandmother pointed to the office blocks and hotels, remembering the jungle that used to be there, green and cool.

'So fast,' said my grandmother. 'It happened so fast.'

Daniel nodded, as if he could see it too, and was very quiet on the way back down the mountain.

My mother disapproved of this friendship.

'Oh Laila,' she said, when I told her. 'No good will come of it, let me tell you.'

'I'm just showing a guest around our island. There's no harm in it.'

'You will get burned, little bird.'

'No, I won't.' I folded my arms and glared at her.

'What would your father say?' she sighed.

She still speaks about my father as if he was able to form opinions about things, although it's five years since his accident.

'Too many cars,' observed the policeman who came to tell us about the crash, nodding to me as I held my mother's head in my hands.

The autumn after my father died the rain fell so hard that I thought it would break through the roof. I sat for hours in my room, watching the trees bending down to the ground. When the clouds parted, a mist would rise like breath and I would watch the rain's oily trails run down the window, until the storm began again.

I wanted Daniel to see the same dangerous deluge this season. But as the days went by and the rains didn't come, he lost interest. Heat and dust came instead and fumes sucked in from forest fires. All the guests suffered, but I only noticed Daniel, wiping sweat from his top lip over and over again, hunched in his chair, until his time came to leave and he waved at me from the foyer as he dragged his suitcase outside.

We are still waiting for the rains. I keep hoping they will arrive violently, so that the news channels film the devastation and maybe Daniel will see it on TV and come back, sit in his usual chair and look out at the monsoon. Of course, I know he is not coming back. It is just a thought that keeps slipping into my mind.

On my days off I take the bus and go up into the mountains again, finding the same spot where I stood with Daniel and my grandmother. The air is cooler up there, but it still carries a tang of dust and ash, as if a hot wave has run up the side of our island, carrying debris.

Yesterday I noticed flying ants in the air, but only a few, going in different directions. Normally, the ants will swarm on the same hot day, just before the storms, but this season, they are uncertain. I watched them as they flew here and there on their damp wings, with no direction or purpose. They still want to time their lives by the rhythm of droughts and storms, heat and growth. They want to see their future clearly, have some hope and fly towards it. As we all do.

UGLY AS SIN *and other clichés*

Out of Sight, Out of Mind

Sue Wright

When Charles pushed Wilhelmina out of the car and drove on, his rear view mirror showed her sitting in the road brandishing two fingers. He put his foot down and rounded the bend until she was well out of sight. Unfortunately, not entirely out of mind.

As it happened, it was a quiet road and she had plenty of time to gather her wits and her belongings before rising to her feet and limping to the verge. Brushing herself down as best she could, she let out an involuntary curse at the large hole in her black tights. There were also ugly scratches on the surface of her green velvet shoes and she was missing an earring.

Her facial expression was not easy to read. The glint in her eyes might have been due to anger but it could equally well have been satisfaction or perhaps it was more like glee. She wiped her fingers in the dew of the grass before running them through her hair and shaking her head to show her auburn tresses to best advantage. She arranged herself atop the five bar gate, drew her warm shawl around her shoulders against the chill of the October morning and waited. There was a serenity about her that was at odds with her circumstances. From time to time she touched her ear where the missing earring should have been and made a wry face.

The sun had by now risen just above the hedge, and turned everything golden, so when the lorry driver came round the corner, dazzled by the low light, what he saw was a flame-haired goddess descend from the sky. He swerved and almost collided with a motorbike coming the other way but managed to stop. His wing mirror showed him a vision of loveliness walking along the verge towards him.

When she arrived alongside the cab, he leaned out of his window, wide eyed and open mouthed. Since he was rendered speechless, it was Wilhelmina who spoke.

'Any chance of a lift?'

He swallowed before replying, 'Where to my lovely?'

She winced for a fraction of a second at his choice of words before bestowing him with a wide smile, climbing into the cab and gesturing forward. Since she chose to stay silent and he remained dumbstruck, the journey seemed longer than it might have done. However, at the first set of red traffic lights, Wilhelmina disembarked. It happened so quickly and silently that it was only when the lights turned green that the lorry driver realised she had gone. He wondered if he had imagined the whole thing;

perhaps he had conjured her into being after a lonely night's driving. It really was time for a coffee break.

Charles was at home, worrying, clock watching, showering and dressing for work. How rash he had been to go to a party on a week night. Angry with himself he was clumsy and made a mess of shaving. One side of his face retained clumps of unshaven shadow, giving him an unkempt look. In fact when Charles finally arrived at the office, several people asked if he was OK, to which he merely scowled.

Wilhelmina had definitely got under his skin. Tired and befuddled, he tried to recall the exact circumstances of the night before. He hadn't noticed her during the evening. Had she been there at all? It was only as he was leaving that she had appeared beside him and asked for a lift. He had never seen anyone quite so beautiful, he was entranced. To begin with the drive was uneventful but about half a mile before they had reached the awkward narrow bend in the road he had glanced across at her for at least the thirteenth time.

The creature sitting beside him was certainly not the angelic beauty that had asked him so sweetly for a lift. This was a wizened crone with a toothless grin and one eye hanging loose from its socket who let out a cackling laugh at his horrified face. Desperate to get her out of his sight and out of his car, he had reacted without thought and he had driven home alone at considerable speed, keeping a wary eye on the rear-view mirror.

Now in the light of a normal day at the office, he wasn't sure what crime he might have committed. Fear and guilt consumed him and he wondered if he was going mad. Had she been a weird hallucination? He spent a long day staring at paperwork, unable to proceed with any work because everything he looked at was superimposed with that face. He sat for a long time with his head in his hands before finally giving up and heading back to his car for the journey home.

He felt some trepidation as he crossed the car park. Gingerly he slid into the driver's seat but recoiled at the sight of something lying on the passenger seat. It was a small silver earring in the shape of a cat and a tiny coil of red hair. He fumbled to open the door but managed to flick them away. Making sure the doors were all locked, he drove home. Had he stopped to look, he might have seen the strand of hair coil around the earring and he might also have watched it lift up and away, swooping gently on the prevailing air currents glinting under the streetlights.

At the moment when Charles was brushing the earring and the strand of hair out of his car, Wilhelmina felt a sting on the crown of her head and ran her hand over the place and put a finger against her ear. She was in a first class train carriage rattling its way south. Although first class was barely preferable to any other carriage, at least she had it to herself. By the time she reached the coast, and walked out into the evening, she was feeling right with the world.

She took a walk through the mist along the sea front, breathing in the last of the day and as the street lights began to flicker on, she took a shortcut through a narrow alleyway towards the rather oddly named Cauldron Cottage. The front window was adorned with cobwebs and in the centre of the sill was a large carved pumpkin with eyes aflame. Just as she was about to enter the door, a faint tinkling sound could be heard. She held out a hand and a small earring entwined with hair rose up from the doorstep and twirled its way into her palm from whence she returned it her ear. As she crossed the threshold, she clicked her fingers and looked around for the cat.

A similar sound was heard by Charles, who had just reached home himself. He was rummaging in the depths of his pocket for his door-key when he heard it. He turned but no-one was there.

Before he could put his key in the lock, the door swung open and he was aware of feeling nervous. When he was confronted by a large black cat with arched back and extended claws he actually let out a squeal. He sidled into the living room, narrowly missing a mauling as he shut the door behind him and leaned on it. There was an eerie light that came from a guttering candle and a smell of something pungent that he couldn't identify.

Whether it was his anxious panting breath that blew out the candle or a gust of wind from the open window was impossible to tell. The ensuing darkness was relieved by a glimmer of light that brightened the eastern sky. Charles leaned on the window sill and watched the full moon slowly emerge from behind a cloud. A rust coloured wisp drifted across its surface, which prompted him to wring his hands. Behind him, the door flew open and slammed against the wall. He spun round to see his favourite picture slide down the wall and smash. An ungodly howl rent the air, but the cat was nowhere to be seen.

A Picture Paints a Thousand Words

Dawn Wyndham

I don't know where the carers found it, this perfect black and white line drawing, possibly an old photograph, modified and printed from a laptop. I look down on the illustration of a house in front of me.

Our house.

They brought it to my table, moved my canes out of the way and presented it to me triumphantly along with brushes and paints. (I used to be a painter, once.)

This is the room he had as his own, filled with maps and books and pin-ups of girls.

I start to colour the curtains.

(Blue, weren't they?)

My mind returned to the day he announced he was going to join up, he and his friends all together. Then the day he left through the back door.

(Colour it red.)

His mother and me, so proud. She was trying to hide her tears, smiling through them as he disappeared, waving, around the corner.

I paint the tree where I used to push him on his swing.

(Colour it green.)

Did it have white blossom? I can't quite recall.

This is the window where, if you'd looked through it that night you would have seen us both huddled round the radio, listening urgently, intensely for news of the front.

I look at the building in the picture and I can't breathe. My heart clenched, my stomach clenched, my teeth, throat and eyes all clenched at the memory – at the pain.

This is the door they came to, and knocked on, before handing me the telegram.

(Colour it black.)

In my head I can see the mud; hear the shrieks, see the pistol he held; as an officer unable to shoot to kill until he was at closer range than his men.

I hear the whistles blowing.

This is the building we lived in and loved.

(Colour it gone.)

Forgive and Forget

Dawn Morgan

The impossibility of making himself known to her, without feeling certain they had been introduced before, caused Henry's hand to shake as he lifted the porcelain teacup to his lips. The brew was too hot, and he burned his mouth, clattering the cup down into the saucer and splashing much of its contents onto the lace tablecloth. He glanced around to see if anyone had noticed his clumsiness and saw that several ladies had turned their heads towards him, teacups and morsels of cake held in the air. But not the lady in question. She continued to gaze absently at the road outside from her table by the window. Carts and carriages rattled past and villagers strolled or rushed along, but she showed no interest in any particular one of them.

In the ten minutes that he had been watching her, she had stared through the leaded panes as if in a trance and only shown animation once, when the clock on the mantelpiece struck three, and her head turned towards it. He had the chance to see her face more clearly then and was very taken with it. Her skin was so fine it was almost translucent, particularly pale on her eyelids, which drooped in a delectable way.

Her lips were red and warm as a ripe plum and her hair very dark. A curl of it had escaped from her hat and dangled over her temple. Henry found himself aching to touch it, and then flushed at the temerity of his thoughts.

He had met her before, he was sure. He remembered every detail of that face. But her name? The place and the occasion? They had gone. If he could only recall her name, he could step over to her, re-introduce himself and blunder and bluff his way through the rest, allowing the lady to fill in the details that hadn't lodged themselves in his brain. But he could do nothing without her name.

'Will you be wanting more tea, sir?' asked the waiting girl.

She had something of a smirk of her face as she placed the tray on the table and reached over to take his cup and teapot, eyeing the stained tablecloth and the brown puddle in his saucer.

'Yes, I will have another pot, thank you,' he said.

She took a small notebook from her apron pocket and lay it on the table to write down his order.

'Any cake sir?' she asked.

She made the proposition sound disgraceful, and he almost considered it, before shaking his head. He was not a lover of cake, having attended too many weddings, funerals and christenings. Joyful or mournful, these occasions were all accompanied by cake.

'No, thank you,' he told her, and watched as she

added the words 'NO CAKE' to her notebook, an inexplicable action that caused him to furrow his brow and look more closely at what she had written.

His name was pencilled clearly at the top of the page, below which were the words 'the curate' in brackets. As she tucked the pad and pencil into her pocket and picked up the tray, he had an idea, so exciting that he began to tremble.

'Excuse me,' he said, plucking at her apron as she turned away.

'Is there something else, sir?' she said sharply, looking down at his hand.

'Oh, I beg your pardon,' he said, flushing again and removing his hand. She was holding the tray so close to his head that a swift jerk of it would have brained him. 'No, no,' he added, in a lowered voice, 'I just wanted to ask you a question.'

'Sorry sir. You'll have to speak up, I can't hear you.'

With a grimace of discomfort, he spoke a little louder.

'I would like to know the name of the lady sitting by the window,' he said. 'I have quite forgotten it.'

'That's Mrs Dalby,' she answered, much more loudly than he had asked.

'Thank you, thank you. Of course it is.'

'Will there be anything else, sir?'

'No, not at all, thank you.'

The girl turned away, her eyes drifting downwards to her pocket, and he suspected she would add some other unflattering detail to her notebook as soon as her hands were not encumbered by his crockery. But then she was gone, and he returned his thoughts to the lady.

So, she was Mrs Dalby, not Miss. Did that matter? Yes, of course it mattered. But should that prevent him from stepping over and paying his respects. No, not at all, though it would beg the question of why he hadn't given attention to the other ladies in the room, some of whose names he remembered perfectly well. But Mrs Dalby was alone and might welcome conversation. To add naturalness, he could speak to her as he was leaving, when he was obliged to pass by her chair. But then he remembered, he had ordered more tea, and the lady might have finished her own before his was even served.

He felt his head become crowded and noisy, like a vessel filled with the sea, and he was uncomfortably hot in his coat. He saw the lady glance at the clock again, which had chimed the quarter hour. She seemed restless and made several little movements that suggested she was about to leave.

Taking a breath of air so deep that it made him dizzy, he got up and walked to her table.

'Ah hem,' he said, tapping his curled fist to his mouth before bending at the waist to speak. 'I hope you are well today, Mrs Dalby. It has been too long since I had the pleasure of seeing you.'

She looked up and he noticed that her eyes were the most remarkable shade of blue, with a dewy lustre as if filled with emotion. She seemed confused.

'It's Mr Nightingale,' he said, giving a half bow. 'The curate.'

'Yes,' she said simply, with a frown.

He licked his lips, cleared his throat again. This was dreadfully awkward, but he had no choice but to press on.

'I trust you are well,' he said, with a cheerful nod. 'And Mr Dalby too.'

She didn't answer, but her frown increased, and he was aware that the sounds of conversation around them had dimmed. The waiting girl arrived at the table in a fluster, though not at any signal from the lady.

'Will there be anything else, ma'am?' she asked.

'No, thank you. I was just leaving.'

Mrs Dalby fumbled for her purse, counting out coins onto the table, then rose, forcing Henry to step back. As she left, Henry went to lift his hat, but it was still on a chair under his table, so his hand fell uselessly to his side. After the door had closed behind her, Henry's shoulders sank and he turned away, to find that half the customers in the tearoom had their eyes on him, most of them unfriendly.

An urge to escape gripped him, but he must go back for his hat and his unpaid bill. Keeping his eyes on the floor he returned to his seat just as the waiting girl returned with his full teapot.

The look she gave him was rather stern and he felt obliged to sit down and pour himself a cup. After blowing at the brown liquid and putting the edge of the cup to his lips, he placed it down again, dropped half a crown on the table and left.

He had not gone ten yards when he heard the waiting girl's voice in the street behind him.

'Mr Nightingale, you have forgotten your hat,' she called, standing on the tearoom doorstep with no apparent intention of going any further.

His face pink, he walked back to her and took the object, mumbling his thanks before continuing on his way.

It was when he stopped to place his hat on his head, looking at his reflection in the draper's window, that he remembered where he had first seen Mrs Dalby. His hands shook on the brim of his hat as he recalled the scene. He had helped the rector to bury her husband six weeks before.

A spasm of self-disgust passed through him, so strong that it resembled nausea, and he leaned his hand against the warm stone of the window surround, his hat sliding to one side, giving his reflection a drunken look.

'Oh Lord, what must she think of me?' he breathed.

Toxins of various sorts passed around his bloodstream and he felt each one separately as he shook with shame and then remorse. He considered calling on her immediately to explain his mistake. Or he could drop a note of apology through her door. But neither action would reduce the pain he had caused her, or his shame.

He walked on miserably, soon finding himself outside the church, without any conscious intention of going there. Entering through the side door, he hung his hat in the vestry and felt the cool, musty air of his workplace clearing his thoughts. He must find some way to make amends, not just to salve his conscience, but to soothe Mrs Dalby's grief. Reflecting on that sentiment, he passed through the studded wooden door into the nave of the church and then stopped, holding his breath. There was Mrs Dalby, alone at the end of a pew, her head bowed, her sobs audible. A shock of alarm shivered through Henry's slight frame and he put his hand behind him to the iron ring of the door. But before he could slip away, she looked up, keeping her eyes on his face for several seconds before bowing her head again.

There was nothing for it but to go to her, and after standing uncertainly for a few moments, he went and crouched beside her pew.

'I am so terribly sorry,' he said.

She continued to sob, the wretched sounds echoing around the vaulted roof.

'I have a terrible memory,' he breathed, the words slipping out of him.

The rhythm of her sobs was unchanged, and he doubted that she'd heard him. He had no notion of how to comfort her and he looked up for inspiration, glancing at the stained-glass window, where Jesus was laying a hand on John's head. The image of the rector came to mind, placing his hand delicately on the arm of a grieving parishioner, and with a sense of unworldliness, as if the limb he watched was not his own, he reached out and lay his own hand on Mrs Dalby's shoulder.

The effect was instant. The lady seemed to collapse against him, and without knowing how the manoeuvre was managed, he found himself in the pew beside her while she let her grief run over his coat.

He sat rigid, his fists against the wood of the pew as she dampened his lapel, her head lying so close to his face that the tendril of hair he had found so attractive was an inch from his lips. Trembling, he mouthed a silent prayer.

Lord forgive me, for I am weak. Lord pity my weakness. Lord give me strength.

He looked up again for help, sending his appeal straight through the roof into the firmament. Seconds later, with a shock, he had his answer. She had come to the church to seek comfort, while he had come with his heart full of the desire to soothe her. And here they sat. And there were his arms, stiff and unused, and now, with a shudder of anticipation, he placed them around her. The timbre of her tears changed instantly to a dull throb, like a child who has been lifted from a cot, and he gazed wonderingly at her hair, his breath disturbing the curl that lay on her temple. And just for a second, a strand of it brushed against his lips.

Ugly as Sin

Sue Wright

In the far corner of the graveyard, Celeste kept a wary eye on the bees that were methodically working their way around a purple buddleia that had seeded itself in a cracked tombstone. Seated on a broken wooden bench while she waited for her sister, she swung her legs, in a soothing rhythmic movement, in time with the distant booming voice of the preacher inside the church, who was building up into a frenzy of declamation.

'...thou shalt not...'

'...repent or perish...'

'...abhore evil...'

'...the wages of sin is death...'

The words held no meaning for Celeste other than serving as a reminder to keep out of sight of the side door that led into the Sunday School. Right now, her sister was inside the sweetshop opposite the church deciding how best to spend their collection money. On sunny Sundays the girls much preferred to daydream away their afternoons until teatime. When Justine returned with her ill-gotten gains the sisters were silent for a while, busily licking brightly coloured sticky lollipops.

Celeste looked up at the gargoyles positioned at strategic points just below the roof. Tentatively, she poked out her tongue in the direction of the one on the corner. It may have been a trick of the light but it seemed to her that his head turned just a little in her direction. She did it again and this time she was sure his head was now pointing directly towards her. A third time provoked a long stone tongue to reach out of his mouth and arch towards her exposing a row of pointed teeth behind his upper lip which was now creased into a snarl. She blinked and looked again but his face was staring into the distance as it had done before.

She looked towards the next one which had a wide grin on his impish face. He looked weary rather than amused - as if his mouth had got stuck like that. She drew her mouth in a wide grin to match, stuck her thumbs in the corners of her mouth and waggled her fingers at him, but nothing happened. Screwing up her face against the brightness of the sun, she did it again – and was almost sure that he winked at her. She did it a third time to be certain before nudging her older sister.

'Who are they?'

'Who?'

'Those people up there under the roof?'

'They're not people, silly, they're gargoyles.'

'That one winked at me and that one on the corner stuck his tongue out at me.'

'Oh don't start that again.'

'What?'

'Making up stories.'

'I'm not.'

'Well they're made of stone, they can't move.'

'Well they did.'

'If you carry on telling lies all the time, you'll end up looking like that. Telling lies is a sin.'

'What's a sin?'

'It is another word for wicked.'

Moving her lollipop to the other hand, she pointed a sticky finger up to the impassive stone faces.

'That's probably how they got to be so ugly in the first place, telling lies.'

Celeste poked Justine in the ribs.

'Anyway, what about buying sweets with the Sunday School money?'

'Don't be such a baby, that's completely different.'

'How is it different?'

'It just is, that's all.'

The voices of the choristers rose and fell, the organ boomed and the mingled sounds soared upwards towards heaven. The lowering sun cast a ray along the roofline and two pairs of stone eyes glittered.

The bees were silent.

A slow grinding sound increased in volume as the giant stone wings of the gargoyles began to unfurl. They were on the move. Swooping like an express train, the wind in their wake was so strong that

Celeste was knocked off the bench and found herself sitting on the grass. Justine dropped the bag of sweets and covered her ears. The gargoyles took up their positions and waited, penning the girls in between the bench and a huge stone cross.

The bees resumed their work and the gargoyles stared at the girls with impassive faces. Celeste picked herself up from the grass and accidentally touched a scaly claw. The gryphon waggled his toes. He didn't exactly smile because his face wasn't the right shape for smiling but Celeste decided that his eyes were friendly. She watched while he preened the feathers of his stone wing and she plucked up the courage to ask the question that had been with her since she had first noticed them.

'Why are you ugly?'

Justine recoiled and put her hand over her own mouth and was astonished when he answered.

'Because we are here to scare people.'

'But why?'

'Our job here is to scare away anything wicked and sinful.'

Celeste's eyes widened and she whispered.

'Am I wicked and sinful?'

'What do you think?'

'I'm not sure.'

He put his head on one side and raised an eyebrow.

Justine picked up the bag of sweets.

The biggest gargoyle licked his lips and stared.

Celeste took the bag from her sister and held it out towards the gargoyles. The gryphon clasped it in his claw and opened it up with his beak, eventually extracting a rather large gobstopper and rolling it round his tongue. The imp with the wide grin picked out a handful of jellybeans and put them all in his mouth at once, rolling his eyes as he chewed, which made both the girls laugh. He put a finger to his nose and tapped. Then he winked.

Hearing the chatter of the congregation coming out of the church, the gargoyles returned to their celestial places. As the girls made their way back towards the church door, Celeste was sure she could still hear stone jaws chewing and sucking, but perhaps it was just the bees.

UGLY AS SIN *and other clichés*

Bag and Baggage

Kathy Miles

It's cold when she gets to Tegel Airport, wind slicing her thin fleece, but the sun is trying its best. Hilda drags her bags into the entrance. She's never believed in travelling light. She has 10 small blue bags, all filled to bursting, carefully tied together so they look like one enormous knobbly piece of luggage. It was a trick she'd learned early on in India, but in those days she was young and fit and now she is old and arthritic, her hands don't work properly, and the bags keep falling over. In addition to the mountain of blue bags, she has two plastic bags which clink as she walks, and a raffia 'bag for life' from the Reichelt supermarket. She'd put wheels on the base of two of the blue bags, a Heath Robinson affair knocked up from an old suitcase she'd found abandoned on the Friedrichstraße. It all threatens to tip over with every step, but she balances the loose bags on the top, and eventually manages to get them onto a baggage trolley. She shuffles to the coffee bar with her improbable load teetering wildly. Once there, she rests it against the table.

She looks for a waitress, but they ignore her. 'Eine

tasse kaffee,' she says hopefully, in her best English accent. Nobody responds. Hilda has never found it easy to attract people's attention. A small unremarkable child, she is now an unremarkable old woman, with short grey hair and glasses that threaten to slide off with every step. At this serving counter she always finds that whole planeloads of passengers get served with cheese rolls or croissants whilst she's continually overlooked, peering over the counter like a tiny, indignant bird. It's as if she doesn't exist. Her temper slowly boils until she angrily grabs the arm of one of the girls.

'Eine tasse kaffee,' she repeats, only adding the 'bitte' when the girl gives her a look of contempt. But it works this time. The coffee is hot and warming, but she's still shaking with cold and anger even after half of it is drunk. The anger wins.

'Bastards,' she shouts out suddenly, her voice ringing across the café. 'Fuckers. Who do you think you are?' A couple of people look at her: most keep their heads bent firmly over their coffee. The manager hurries over.

'Bitte lassen.' He looms over her menacingly. Hilda squints at him flirtatiously. 'Entschuldigung,' she says apologetically. He repeats his request and starts to move her bags away from the table. Hilda sighs. It's time she left, in any case. She still hasn't checked on her flight.

There are no seats left on the 14.55 Lufthansa flight to Zurich. Hilda slams her hand on the desk in

frustration. The man behind the desk rolls his eyes-
Hilda is not an easy customer- and suggests she tries
Schönefeld instead; there is, he believes, a late-
afternoon flight she could take.

'And how the hell do you expect me to get all
these to Schönefeld?' Hilda indicates her baggage,
which is already wilting off the Tegel trolley. She adds
a few more swear words for good measure. The man
shrugs and turns to the next customer. Hilda wants to
let loose a torrent of the most vivid and
comprehensive language she can muster. She wants to
cast doubt on this man's parentage, on the parentage
of his children, his ancestry, and his mother's
reputation. But her German is flagging, and she's not
been able to afford breakfast, so instead she snorts,
and seats herself near the departure board to consider
her options. There's a flight leaving for Berne at 5
pm, or she can nip onto an internal flight for Munich
at 3. But she really wanted to go to Zurich today.
Irritation ripples through her. She sizes up those in
the waiting area: a woman wearing a cerise and
turquoise striped jumper with matching cerise-and-
gold-earrings; a pretty Chinese girl in a black jacket
talking into her phone; a couple of travel-stained
English tourists in duffle coats, their holdalls bulging
with shopping, and two security guards in blue
trousers and shirts, pistols in their holsters. She looks
away. The sky is clear and flat over the airport, but
snow clouds are rolling slowly in from the east. Hilda
watches as the 11.30 from Heathrow noses into its

docking point at the gate; businessmen and tourists pour off, an untidy rabble of bags, briefcases and rucksacks.

13.00 hours and the plane from Schiphol is delayed. Hilda taps her hand impatiently on the metal bar of her seat. This plane is almost never late. Perhaps a strike, she thinks, a security alert, you never know these days. The scheduled flights from Frankfurt and Madrid have also been delayed, but she sees a big Airbus touching down, rolling itself smoothly onto the runway. Tegel is her favourite airport. Like her, it is old, a bit scruffy round the edges, struggling to cope with all its baggage. By rights she should not be here today. None of them should. Tegel should already have closed, to make way for the new Berlin Brandenburg complex. But the work has been delayed, so she sinks back in her seat, grateful that, for now, she can sit here and watch planes skimming in and out like dragonflies landing on a pond.

Hilda has a passion for flying. When other people are gripping the seats in terror at take-off and landing, she is glued to the window, loving the acceleration of the plane, waiting for the lift-off that will take them high up into the sky, as if the earth is no longer able to keep the plane fixed to the ground. She remembers the last flight she took; was it last year, the year before, twenty years ago? Her mind wanders these days, plays stupid tricks on her, so that she has no control over her memories, and sometimes, over what she says or does. But the last flight, she remembers that.

It was when she came to Berlin, Stockholm to Schönefeld. It was a good journey: no turbulence, and a nice in-flight meal, meatballs with small rounds of potato and vegetables. She'd saved hard to afford the ticket, stashing up kronas one by one until she had enough, not eating for days at a time. But it had been worth it. Sweden had lost its charm; its people were not as generous as Berliners.

It's the clouds she recalls most about that flight. They were like the wraps of fabric laid on the floor to make her sister's wedding dress, that hot Jaipur summer; big white fluffy clouds, thick, dense and lacy. In places they were ridged, little buttons of cloud imprinted like footprints on the main belt of cumulus, so that you wondered who had walked across them. And later, when the sunset came, they looked like the bolts of silk that were dyed in big vats in Jaipur; and when the sun started to fade from the massive swathe of sky, the colours changed to bruised blues and purples, and Hilda knew those colours, too. That was the best flight of all, she thinks now, and wishes she was already queuing in the departure lounge, boarding pass in hand, the excitement of the journey to come.

Hilda's father had been a textiles exporter who had moved himself and his family to India in the early 1930s in search of better things; Hilda had been born there, in the new Sawai Man Singh Hospital. She doesn't remember the hospital of course. But she

does remember her father's office, with its big cooling
fans and ice machine, pots of aloe vera and japonica.
She and her sister Margaret would sometimes be
allowed to play in the grounds outside the office or
shop in the local markets with their ayah. Margaret
was much older than her, but Hilda was never made
to feel she was unwanted or in the way. But then
everything changed. Her father's exporting business
failed, and shortly afterwards, the family returned to
England, leaving Margaret there with her new
husband. That was the last Hilda had seen of her
sister. Her father too, because as soon as they got
back home – though to Hilda, home had been the
hot, vibrant streets of Jaipur, and England a strange,
cold, foreign place – he left them. Their mother,
embittered and angry, didn't mention him again, and
Hilda was afraid to ask. India and her father were in
the past, and the past was a country they never set
foot in. Hilda was sent to boarding school, where the
girls bullied her; she spent her days longing for her
old school friends, for the noisy, colourful country
she had left, for the animals and insects and
suffocating heat. She had been a clever girl, but
didn't complete her schooling, leaving early to work
in an office. There had been a marriage - brief, lonely
- but no children. Jobs, but no career. Drifting, she
thinks now, I was always a drifter; always wanting to
be somewhere else. Over the years she has lived in
France and Sweden and Spain, taken bar jobs in

Majorca and Tenerife, worked as a cleaner in Italy, a nanny in Greece, paying her way round the world but never making enough to settle down. Not India though. She had never returned there, although Margaret would have been pleased and surprised to see her. She doesn't even know whether Margaret is still alive, and now, at 79, she's in Berlin, with a bad arm and hands that don't work properly and legs that give way on her in the cold. Still drifting.

She loves Berlin at this time of year. The Christmas markets, full of noise and music and the smell of bratwurst and gluhwein, tourists jostling at the stalls to buy gloves and scarves and decorations, purses shoved carelessly into their pockets for anyone to see. At the Alexanderplatz this year they were roasting a whole pig, his body revolving slowly on the spit, eyes glazed with the reflection of the fire. She'd found enough money for a pork roll and a mug of gluhwein, and turned the taste of it round and round in her mouth. Other stalls were selling plates of fried potatoes or cabbage, bowls of goulash soup, and the gluhwein mugs were embellished with the name and date of the market. Hilda noticed how many of the tourists slipped the empty mugs into their pockets when they had finished. It was a game between stallholder and customer, a kind of legalised stealing; the stallholders knew the mugs wouldn't be returned, and put a deposit charge on them. Hilda liked the thought of stealing being legitimised here, provided for, expected from you. It made everything so much easier. But she had no need of pretty gluhwein mugs and gave hers carefully back to the stallholder, receiving the precious euros in exchange.

The 13.00 flight from Schiphol is finally announced. There's a sudden frisson of excitement, as passengers start to gather up bags and children, point to the arrivals board, jabber at each other in Dutch and German. It will be a good while yet, Hilda thinks, before they can board. Nevertheless, a straggle of them head at speed for the departure gate, knocking other passengers out of the way and leaving behind half-eaten sandwiches, newspapers and packets of crisps. Hilda sidles over to one of the tables and removes several of these, along with a glossy magazine. As she goes back to her seat, a red and silver Air Berlin glides to a halt on the runway, sleek and graceful as a shark. She opens the magazine and looks at the pictures: immaculate women posed with expensive handbags, adverts for perfumes and gold jewellery. A different world.

It's 6 pm and Hilda wakes with a start. She has nodded off for several hours. Panicking, she looks for her bags, and sighs with relief. Everything she owns is in those bags. Her few clothes, some books and reminders of the places she has visited; a small pottery jar from Italy, cheap necklaces and bracelets, a coffee mug, some soap, a woollen blanket bought in Greece, a sleeping bag, torn and faded now, but still warm enough if she wraps herself in the blanket first, a torch without the battery, and some aluminium cooking pots, their sides dented from travelling.

She realizes suddenly that a security guard is standing over her, his face screwed up as if there's a bad smell under his nose. He asks her to leave, in careful, impeccable German. Hilda pretends not to understand and answers him in Swedish. The guard asks her again, not quite so politely this time. His hand hovers casually on his holster. He's recognised me, Hilda thinks, he knows who I am.

'Scheiße', she yells at him. She looks through the windows of Tegel, at the snow that is just starting to fall. It's going to be cold tonight. The security guard waits as she collects her lump of blue bags, her clinking carriers, and rearranges the big worn boots with no laces. She'll have to get the bus back into town now, get off at Hauptbahnhof or Tiergarten. She scrabbles in her pocket for a few remaining euros, but the guard is ahead of her and slips a 10 euro note into her hand. It makes her angry, but she's too tired to argue. There's a railway arch at Tiergarten, out of the wind, somewhere the Landespolizei won't notice her. She can come back to Tegel tomorrow, as she does every day, to watch the planes taking off and landing, with their promise of far places, different horizons, some kind of future.

One day she will go to Zurich, when she's saved up enough euros. One day.

First published in The Lonely Crowd, 2015

UGLY AS SIN *and other clichés*

It's All Gone Tits Up

Sue Wright

'Is that Sid's taxis?'

'Yes Ma'am, at your service. What can I do for you today?'

'Do you think that you might be prevailed upon to take myself and two friends for a short trip this afternoon? I would like to visit the tea room on the promenade where I have reserved a table for afternoon tea at four o'clock.'

'Right-oh Mrs. What's the address?'

'My name is 'Miss' Proctor and you may collect us from the vicarage at 3.40.'

There was a flippancy about his tone which niggled her. She was, after all, the daughter of a vicar, and there were standards to uphold. It was a matter of principle, and her principles were concerned above all with respectability.

'Birthday is it?'

His presumption was such that she almost wished that he would dare to ask her age so that she could give him a piece of her mind. As it happened, he did not, because he already knew she was eighty. He knew

145

because his wife was a member of the WI and she knew everything that was going on in the village. Sid had heard a great deal about Miss Proctor, most of it bizarre.

She lived alone in the old vicarage with nothing but a budgerigar for company. Apparently it was pretty much as it had been when the vicar was still alive; a huge rambling place with stone floors and threadbare carpets. It had been rather grand in its day by all accounts and there were few modern amenities. Her only concession to the advance of technology was a push button telephone on the mahogany table in the hallway which she preferred to cover with an embroidered table cloth.

The pictures on the wall behind the table had been in their places for more than seventy years. She supposed that moving them would have revealed un-faded wallpaper squares which simply would not do. It bothered her that the display was well past its best, many of the frames were crooked and their silver was tarnished. There were sepia portraits of ancient relatives, biblical quotes in cross stitch, a few church dignitaries carrying bibles (in colour), and a black and white photograph of a Sunday School outing to the seaside.

It was this picture that Miss Proctor's eyes rested on while she waited for the taxi. There was a row of moustached men in three piece suits sitting on the sand, leaning against the sea wall, looking hot and serious; there were ladies in polka dot frocks and wide brimmed hats fussing over children and smiling towards the camera. Most of the children wore knee length bathing suits, boys and girls alike.

One child, still wearing her ordinary clothes and shoes could be seen walking into the sea. The sound of the surf had drowned out the angry shouts from the beach and the young Miss Proctor had waded up to her shoulders in the water. She let herself lift and float with an unaccustomed sense of freedom. She was actually a good swimmer and had won prizes at the school swimming gala. However, after this transgression, she had not been allowed to go on the annual seaside trip again.

The sound of voices outside the house and a short blast from a car horn interrupted her reverie.

When the three ladies were delivered one minute early to the tearoom, several other members of the WI were already there. They had decorated the table with home-made bunting and tied two large pink and silver helium balloons emblazoned with an eight and a zero to a paperweight. Miss Proctor was aghast at the spectacle but she reminded herself of her father's constant admonition to be gracious towards parishioners and forced her face into a smile and her mouth into a 'thank you'. One's duty was always more important than personal considerations after all.

She did approve of the neat black dress and white frilled apron of the waitress who ushered them to their seats, and she admired the three tiered cake stands piled with small triangular sandwiches, miniature scones and iced fancies. She was extremely fond of cake.

The waitress observed the chatter for a while and at an appropriate moment gestured to the pianist whose performance of 'Happy Birthday' was accompanied by the assembled ladies with varying degrees of tunelessness. It was an ordeal for her, but Miss Proctor had managed to smile throughout and was now enjoying a salmon and cucumber sandwich and eyeing an iced bun. Feeling a little uncomfortable around her midriff, she loosened the waistband of her skirt and undid a couple of buttons of her shirt. Concerned that she should manage this surreptitiously, she was concentrating hard, so she didn't notice one of the ladies at the far end of the table whispering to the waitress. She was taken aback when all the teacups were removed and replaced with champagne flutes.

'We thought an 80th birthday called for more than tea so we ordered champagne.'

There was something a little gleeful about the woman who spoke and Miss Proctor looked around in a bit of a fluster. Her usual alcohol consumption was limited to a small sherry at Christmas. In fact the bottle in the cupboard at the vicarage had served her well for several Christmases.

Tentatively she took a sip. All eyes were upon her. She took another and smiled, this time genuinely. After her third glass of champagne she impulsively suggested a short walk along the pier, at which everyone cheered. What with the chattering and the laughter, the walk to the end took a while. The sound of the fairground lent a certain ambiance and Miss Proctor was unusually relaxed.

Sid's car horn went unheard, so he parked the car and strode along the pier towards the gaggle of women.

Whether it was the alcohol, or her eightieth birthday, or the photograph of the Sunday School trip that prompted her to do what she did next, she couldn't be sure. It was just that a little spark of pleasure had arisen for the first time in decades and made her reckless. She laughed as she squeezed her ample frame between the bars of the railing. Sid and the WI ladies watched her plummet rather than dive into the water. The resulting splash was substantial enough to spray them all. Beneath the water, the exertion of swimming strained her remaining buttons to their limit and they popped open one by one. The first thing to breach the surface was her magnificent bosom, for the delectation of the only man who would ever see it.

'Gorblimey - would you look at that!'

UGLY AS SIN *and other clichés*

Counting Sheep

Kathy Miles

It's early when he wakes. Light purls of mist seam the window, like a first foam of milk in the pail. Rhys lies back, enjoying the warm just-woken feeling. Then he remembers. She is coming today. The thought pillows up through the bedclothes and he throws them off, as if they are scalding through his skin. The air tastes cold, but sun is already piercing the clouds with thin strands of saffron. He wants today to be perfect.

In the large tiled kitchen he boils the kettle, puts on eggs and toast, lets Mollie out of the back door to shake the night out of her coat. He looks around in despair. Last night he'd tidied the place, vacuumed the living room, washed and dusted and polished, but in the morning light it looks greasy and faded. Like himself, greying, past its best. She'll know I still live alone, he thinks: the single raincoat hung on the back of the door, boots caked with mud, lines of tinned beans and tomato ketchup in the cupboard. He's tried to keep it nice, *cymhennaidd* his mam would have said. But the days get to you in the end. Dawns and dusks blur in work and weather, so you end up wearing the dust like a favourite sweater. She'll notice all this. She won't stay. He's surprised how much this matters.

Yesterday he'd bought cake and fresh bread, smoked salmon, cheese, and the coffee he remembered was her favourite. Mrs. Williams grinned slyly as he slid his purchases onto the counter.

'Not your usual, Rhys, having visitors are we?'

He'd blushed and swept the items into his bag, suddenly angry at himself for not going to the big Morrisons store in Newtown instead of the local village shop: another twenty miles, but nobody sticking their nose into your business. Now he wonders if he should have got more. Jodie hasn't said what time she's coming. He's assumed she'll want lunch after the long journey, but perhaps he should have put a casserole on, something more substantial. Then again, maybe she won't want to sit at the table with him, maybe she'll just have a coffee and be on her way. He walks uneasily around the kitchen. He doesn't like not knowing. Mollie comes back in, her tail wagging like a flag, and he scoops dogfood and mixer into her bowl, briefly pats her head as she stoops to eat. He wonders if Mollie will remember her. She was only a puppy when Jodie left, but still, dogs have long memories, don't they?

In the study he checks his emails, but there's nothing from Jodie. He'd hoped for a message, just a few lines to say she's looking forward to seeing him again. Perhaps she isn't, and this is just her way of tidying up loose ends. He thinks Jodie must have something important to tell him, otherwise why is she coming after so long? Perhaps she is getting married or - his stomach tightens - that she is ill, dying even, and wants to tell him in person. If it wasn't urgent, she could have emailed or phoned, written a letter. She knows where he lives.

With the back door open, he can smell the earth after last night's heavy rain. Petrichor, he thinks, the word sifting through from somewhere at the back of his mind. The smokey, lanolin scent of sheep drifts from his coat as he stands there. But rain has widowed the air of the meadowsweet and honeysuckle fringing the bank beyond the yard. He wonders if Jodie still remembers those scents, or whether the hot oiliness of the city has masked them into a past she no longer thinks about. Of course, she was never a country girl. When she'd first come to live at Ty Hen she had been shocked and amazed by the old-stone mossy-ness of its walls, the sash windows that always stuck when you opened them, the peeling paintwork and massive dresser in the kitchen. He gave in to her requests for a new bathroom, double glazing, and creamy wallpapers. The house had needed modernizing. But the dresser stayed. Jodie had pleaded with him to get rid of it. 'It's so ugly,' she said, and she was right, it was ugly, a tall monstrosity of a dresser, taking up the whole of one side of the wall. But the dresser had been his mother's pride and joy, and when he inherited Ty Hen, he knew it was the one thing he would keep. So it stood there still, dominating the kitchen space as much as -

in her own way - his mother had done, though now it was filled with books and DVDs instead of her best Sunday china.

The morning is passing too fast. Rhys begins to set the big wooden table with plates and cutlery. He puts the half-empty whisky bottle down into the cupboard, washes last night's glass, and wonders if he should light the fire. It's warmer now, but his mother always lit a fire when they had visitors. Through the open door he can see tree-branches swaying across the valley, flecks of leaves blown up like small squares of paper, each of them carrying a piece of breeze on their surface. He puts on his coat and goes outside to see to the sheep, calling each one by name, checking them over as they run towards him, loving the rustle of their feet, the woolly, whispering sounds they make as they jostle shoulder to shoulder for the grain he brings. It had always been sheep at Ty Hen. His parents had farmed several hundred; good sheep, of sound stock, and they had been lucky enough to win contracts with two large supermarket chains. But these days it was hardly enough to make a living, and Rhys had never wanted to be a farmer. He was a business writer, able to work from home, and when his parents died, he sold the sheep and two of the fields, and moved from his tiny bachelor flat in Cardiff back into Ty Hen. The Jacobs had been Jodie's idea. She saw his restlessness when he looked out at the land. It was as though he was searching for something, as if the landscape was somehow incomplete, the fields yearning for their lost herds. So he had bought 50 Jacobs, and each year, sold the lambs on to other rare-breed enthusiasts, and showed the best of the yearlings at the Royal Welsh. He only has fifteen now. He knows he should get rid of them; they are expensive to keep, and he no longer breeds or shows them. Not since that night. His throat tightens at the memory. The night he failed them.

It had been a late June evening, heat clinging to the ground, little wisps of mist starting to rise from the river. The Jacobs were sleepy, some still grazing the Long Meadow, others lying down in small huddles. Rhys was working in his study finishing an article, aware that the deadline was rapidly approaching and his editor waiting. And then he heard the barking. He stopped typing and put his head on one side to listen, because it wasn't Mollie's voice he could hear. The barks were deep, insistent, with a note of something he couldn't identify, and he was confused as to where they were coming from. Then he heard the sheep, their terrified cries rising on the wind. He'd rushed to the meadow in a panic. It was the blood he saw first, gushing from the ripped throats of two of the ewes. Another sheep struggled to get up, her side gashed, intestines spilling onto the grass. Two of the lambs were already dead, lying in their own blood and faeces; three more bleated pitifully as the dogs slashed and tore at them. They were big dogs, Alsatians or Rottweilers. All Rhys knew was a blur of dark hair against the stark white of the sheep, the terrible noise in his head. He ran to the closest of the dogs and pulled him off with his bare hands, teeth flaying his skin, not noticing the pain. He kicked the dog in the head and it whimpered and sloped off, jaws red and slimy. Then he saw the two men cowering by the hedge, faces a mask of terror. He yelled at them, his voice raw and frantic, and eventually they came, helped him drag off the frenzied animals. He cursed himself for not having brought his gun, blasted the dogs out of existence, the men, too, if he'd had his way. They were shocked, apologetic, guiltily pulled shiny wads of money from their pocket. English tourists, out for an evening stroll in the lane, slipping their dogs from the lead, not aware of the strong, exquisite lure of the sheep beyond the gate. Rhys swore at them until he was hoarse, the pain of his mangled animals making him wild, savage, an unspeakable creature from some dark myth. But it was too late. Nothing would bring back his lost sheep.

He was glad, then, that Jodie hadn't been around. He couldn't have borne her tears. He buried the sheep in anger, and his anger had also been for Jodie, for the way she left him, and he buried his anger deep in the ground with his ewes so that even now, when he stood above the place where they were, he could feel it seeping up through the earth like a fretful spirit. And now she's coming today, and he realizes that even though he's been waiting so long for this day, he doesn't want to see her. Eight years since they last met, and she'll have changed, he thinks, they'll both have changed. There won't be that thing between them anymore, that little pulse connecting them like a silver thread, running between their nerves and arteries so that neither of them had to say out loud what they were thinking.

He had met Jodie at a music festival in Newtown. Mclusky were headlining, along with Ectogram and Budgie: the best of the Welsh bands that year, and he'd bought his ticket early, not wanting to miss the chance to see them play. Jodie had been standing next to him in the damp, muddy field, the crowds pressed so close together that it was impossible to avoid contact. He remembers how she was then: a mane of brown hair clipped back with a hairslide, a red maxi-skirt, and a pink waistcoat with fluffy white sheep appliqued onto the cotton. It was the waistcoat that drew him to her – in the hot noisy atmosphere of the festival, it reminded him of home. He'd chatted to her as they waited for the band to start playing, and afterwards it seemed natural to link arms, wander over to the Beer Tent and continue their conversation. She had come down from Birmingham with a group of friends, and from the first tentative smile, they knew it was special, that she wouldn't go home again. And for five years, she didn't. It was as if Jodie had become his heft, just as much as Ty Hen: in her was everything he had ever wanted or needed. He thought it was the same for her.

She had left so gradually that at first, Rhys didn't realize it was happening. Just that things started to disappear – ornaments, pairs of shoes, photographs- as if the wind were gusting them off one by one. And then one day he opened the wardrobe and found that her clothes had been spelled away, and when he went downstairs, Jodie was standing by the front door, a suitcase beside her, its lock shut tightly as a pursed mouth, a taxi waiting outside. She didn't explain and he didn't ask, not wanting to hear the answer. Another man, he supposed, accepting it in his quiet country way just as he'd accept the death of a new-born lamb. He still doesn't understand why she left. He thinks now that the not-asking and the not-telling may have been the reason. There had been no rows, no discontentment that he had noticed. But the not-noticing, too, there was blame in that, he supposed. Rhys went on with his life the best he could, but there had been no-one else. And now, out of the blue, her email, asking if she can see him.

It's three o'clock when a small blue Fiesta drives into the yard. Rhys panics, unsure what to do. If he opens the door immediately, it looks too desperate. In the end, he hides in the living room, watching from behind the curtains as Jodie gets out of the car, stands looking round the once-familiar yard, taps lightly on the front door. For a moment, he wonders if he should just not answer it, let her drive away without seeing him, but opens the door anyway. The sunshine behind her makes her blurry, as though he can see right through her, a rosary of dawn light ghosting her hair into clouds of smokebush. She moves towards him slightly, and he sees a quick glimpse of pink beneath the brushed cotton of her raincoat. For a second he remembers his anger buried out in the field with the ewes, remembers too the pain in his torn and bitten hands, flesh parting like sliced peaches, raw and visceral.

'Come in Jodie,' he says, and smiles.

UGLY AS SIN *and other clichés*

Home Sweet Home

Dawn Wyndham

Her gentle, elongated face was etched with tiredness. Delayed by giving birth two days ago, she was the last to flee. Amid the flames and smoke billowing around her, she held tight to the branch she hung from, high above a forest floor fanged with charred, fallen trees.

Subdued sunlight shone through her long auburn hair, silhouetting her body in a foggy cloud. Her instincts were sharpened by the coming of morning and she sensed the presence of danger as vividly as carnal pain. Lifting her head to sniff the acrid air, she felt a disturbing change in the rhythm of things and panic began to claim her. The sounds of her baby brought her back to herself. Hearing him keening, she looked down at his tiny new-born face and made gentle hooting noises to calm him. He groped the air, feeling her fear and coughing a terror all his own. Wind snarled at the hot dawn like a sinister red beast, goading the fire on. Something evil was happening.

She searched the trees for a flash of orange, a glimpse of ginger fur, for another of her kind, but the smoke was so thick it was all she could do to keep her streaming eyes open. Although she was accustomed to prowling the forest alone, she sometimes made contact with the congress of orang-utan who lived here, especially the other females with their young. Now with an infant of her own she searched for them. Where were they? She cradled her son, lifting him to her breast to encourage him to latch on and cling more tightly; hoping the act of suckling would soothe him. Skin touching skin, she tenderly stroked his head, still shiny from the pickling of the womb, brushing his singed fluff of hair free of ash. Breathing in as he was breathing out, her keen sense of smell told her of the smoke filling his young lungs. His small hand sought the fur around her neck and he covered her nipple with his mouth and closed his eyes.

She had travelled a long way across the jungle canopy, her seven-foot arm span swinging her effortlessly from treetop to treetop. The new day revealed the fire was at its worst here. At one point yesterday she'd had to descend from the trees to avoid the flames, but the ground had been on fire. As she relived the trial of it, she made small noises and rocked to comfort herself, as she had last night as darkness fell; murmuring ancient sounds only her kin could make in the hollows of their throats and which, somewhere in her head, fathoms deep, she kept close. Her feet and hands had got burned from just the short burst of speed to reach across the clearing and into the forest again with the baby clinging to her back, climbing up and up as if the altitude would cool her blistered limbs. Listening out for the long call of a male orang-utan, she felt the branches for food, but all she found were shriveled leaves. She was hungry. She must eat to have milk for the baby, to have strength to travel.

Which way? She was lost in this place she had always known so well, her mental map of the forest disturbed. She climbed a little higher and gazed across the grey clouds of smoke to the distance. In the faded blue of the far-away she sensed water. It was their only chance. She shouted a loud hoot, listening for the response of an answering call, desperation driving her, instinct and tenacity telling her she would be going in the right direction - towards the river; to the tea-coloured waters that flow in tributaries across Central Kalimantan; to the orang-utan sanctuary where she was raised; to home, to safety.

First published in Zoomorphic Magazine

UGLY AS SIN *and other clichés*

A Change is as Good as a Rest

Sue Wright

Deirdre sat in the corner of the empty carriage. She didn't know that she was alone, for she was fast asleep, gently snoring. Her neck was bent sideways and her head leant against the window. Her open mouth with its little silvery trail of spittle was reflected in the glass. If she had been aware of this she would have moved immediately and begun to rummage in the green leather handbag that was clasped in both hands on her lap. She did a great deal of rummaging in the depths of that green bag and frequently came across some surprising things. Yesterday she had found a half-eaten sandwich, four pieces of Lego and a Christmas card with a photograph of a family she didn't know.

The train gave a jolt and she sat upright, sniffed and peered out of the window into the dark. She had no idea where she was or how long she had been dozing. The train was moving backward and she began to feel anxious. Surely when she got into the train, she had been facing the direction of travel. Why would it now be going backwards? It began to pick up speed and the lights flickered. She blinked a few times and continued to peer out of the window. She reached for her coat on the seat next to her.

Placing her bag down carefully between her feet, she put her arms into the sleeves and wriggled the length of it underneath her so that she could do up the buttons. Feeling in the pockets she found a green bobble hat with a red pompom. She pulled it firmly onto her head and a soft frizz of grey remained outside its confines like a halo. She groped around for her bag and returned it to her lap. She sat bolt upright, gripping the leather handles so hard that her knuckles turned white. The window reflected the line of her nose and jaw, topped with the hat and its surrounding hair. A glance briefly reminded her of her grandmother's cameo brooch that she had admired. Her musing about the brooch was interrupted when the train drew to a squealing halt and the door at the end of the carriage opened to a man in uniform.

'All change.'

Deirdre looked at him but stayed put.

'This train terminates here; you need to get off'.

He walked towards her and she stood up, sidled away from him towards the door and groped for a handle that wasn't there. He leaned across her and pressed the button that released the doors with a loud hiss. She scuttled down onto the platform, nearly losing her balance, but managed to keep on her feet. Her footsteps were brisk as if she knew where she was going until confronted with a green sign she stopped and stared at it before following the direction of its illuminated white arrow. Disconcerted by the darkness, she walked through the unmanned barrier just as the train whooshed away, leaving an eerie silence in its wake.

Deirdre wasn't the sort of woman who could be spooked by an empty station at night so she hooked the handles of her bag over one elbow, patted her head to check her hat, took a deep breath and made her way through a narrow alleyway into the brightly lit street. Dazzled by the unfamiliar glare, she looked this way and that, trying to get her bearings. A clock struck and she counted seven or eight, or maybe it was nine. It was so easy to get muddled.

She thought she recognised the fish and chip shop and crossed the road to peer into its steamy window. Leaning against the glass, she felt the warmth at her back as she reached and clicked the fastener on her bag open. She placed her hand over her mouth while she tried to remember what it was that she needed to find. A man holding a bag of chips came out of the shop and stood next to her. When she looked towards him he winked and offered her a chip. She held the hot chip in her fingers and stared at it until the man nodded at her, then she put it in her pocket and he laughed. She didn't know what was funny but she smiled at him anyway, although she edged a bit further away from him. She waited patiently while he ate all of his chips, and watched as he screwed up the paper and threw it with a practised aim into a nearby bin. As soon as he moved on, she began peering into her bag once more. She had a horrible feeling that something was missing, except that she couldn't remember what it was. Never mind, it would come back to her.

She set off down the street with purposeful steps which gradually grew more hesitant as she walked, until she finally came to a stop, attracted by a brightly lit shop window display. A cluttered group of small electrical items confronted her, wreathed in tinsel and fairy lights. She liked the sparkle and the gleam of chrome with glints of reflected light that bounced from one item to another. She liked the coils of white cable with their square plugs. Everything looked incomprehensibly modern and practical but there were Christmas baubles to fill every remaining space and in the far corner, a large box wrapped with silver and green striped paper and a big red bow.

The shop door opened with a pleasant jangle as a customer came out. The woman looked at Deidre standing there and held the door open for her. She smiled at the woman and entered the shop. It was warm inside and she relaxed a little. There was nobody behind the counter but Deirdre could hear voices in a back room. They were whispering and laughing so she moved closer in order to hear what they were saying. If there was one thing she couldn't stand, it was people talking about her behind her back. The sparkle in the window display caught her eye and she turned to look, the voices forgotten. It was too much to resist, so she reached in and lifted out the big silver box with the ribbon. It was surprisingly light and Deirdre put it on the counter while she undid the ribbon. It was a bit awkward because she still had her bag hanging from one elbow but she persevered. Inside the paper was a plain brown box. It didn't even have a proper lid on it and there was nothing inside. Disappointed, she left the box on the counter and returned to the window display. A shiny red kitchen object with a dial on the front caught her attention and she held it in her hand and twisted the knob. When it suddenly rang loudly she dropped it into her bag, retreated towards the door and walked out of the shop. Behind her, the two shop assistants were staring after her. Deirdre would have been upset to know that they really were talking about her now and even more outraged had she heard the telephone call to the police.

She trudged on as far as a bus stop that she wasn't sure if she recognised. Bus stops all looked pretty much the same really and she didn't have her reading glasses so she couldn't read what it said. She looked both ways up the street but there was no bus to be seen in either direction. She stood for a while shifting her weight from one foot to the other and then sat down on the graffiti covered bench. She waited. She heard the clock chime from time to time and she was already cold by the time the snow began to fall. She looked up at the gathering white, swirling against the dark. It was restful, so peaceful; like being on a

Christmas card.

One by one the shops began to close and the lights went out. A bus came and went but Deirdre's eyes were closed and she didn't get on it. Her hands, still holding the bag, relaxed their grip and the bag fell to the floor unnoticed. Her hat and collar were dappled with snow and she slid sideways across the bench. By the time the policeman tapped her on the shoulder her lips were blue. He called for assistance, picked up her belongings, retrieved the kitchen timer and saw her off into the ambulance when it came.

It was several hours before her eyes opened again and many days before she was ready to get out of bed. When she was eventually well enough, she sat in a chair propped up by cushions with her bag safely on her lap, which became a daily routine until the day she was told that she had a visitor. She was worried about whom it might be and sometimes she forgot people's names, which was embarrassing. The woman who came in was completely unknown to her and at first she seemed rather stern, which put Deirdre on her best behaviour, which was tiring and she struggled to keep awake. When the woman stopped speaking, Deirdre reached over and put a reassuring hand on the woman's arm.

'Thank you for coming dear.'

'Ok then, I'll see you tomorrow when they bring you home.'

'Home?'

Deirdre worried about how she was going to get

home from here but the nice taxi driver that came to collect her seemed to know where he was going. She was surprised when he pulled up outside a big hotel, much like the one in Bognor Regis where she had once been on holiday. When he rang the bell for her, a woman dressed as a nurse came out to help her up the ramp. Perhaps it was some kind of fancy dress event that she had forgotten about.

Her room was small but cosy and there were lots of knick-knacks and pictures of people that Deirdre didn't know. She picked up a little cameo brooch in a glass bowl and ran her finger over the pale face of the lady in profile and wondered who she was. The woman dressed as a nurse came in and helped her into a big armchair and a young man brought her a cup of milky tea and two custard creams. It all felt very restful.

UGLY AS SIN *and other clichés*

Bright Eyed and Bushy Tailed

Dawn Wyndham

The end of the garden is a tangle of brambles and weeds. Jasper Chap was sleeping in his den beneath the neglected garden shed. He stretched and yawned, smacking his lips and pushing his paws through the air in a rather fetching arc. A young adolescent fox with a thick, shiny coat and sleek, white-tipped tail, he was as brilliant and beautiful as jasper, the semi-precious stone his mother had named him after. He opened his amber eyes and then quickly shut them again. Why was there so much light today? Next to him, in his larder hole, was a fine store of take-away food boxes, household rubbish, dead mice, worms, old sandwiches and discarded half-eaten chocolate bars. Jasper had a liking for root vegetables and flower bulbs too, and dug up any he could find in the gardens around his den, making him rather unpopular with the neighbours. Apart from cars and the risk of getting run over, life is easy for *vulpes vulpes* in London.

Half asleep, he thought of when he had left home, with a list of dos and don'ts that stretched on for days. He hadn't seen his parents for years. His mother ran away to join a skulk of foxes in the Cotswolds just after he left. The local poacher writes on her behalf now and again, but of course, being a fox, Jasper can't read, so can't understand a word of what she might be trying to say, but he's sure her messages are full of longing and heartbreak. His father is a beautiful stuffed museum exhibit in the section on flowers, but sometimes moved to be in the fruit section. Dead, of course, but still hauntingly gifted.

Although Jasper could sleep through a hurricane, he was jolted awake by the sound of a shovel digging very near to his den. That's where the light was coming from. He sniffed the air. Something was happening to disturb his peace. Something was very wrong.

Jocelyn Oftentimes and her father, Professor Cyrus Oftentimes stood at the window of their third floor flat in the Victorian mansion that had once been a single family home. It was divided into six flats now with the veterinary practice that was the Professor's vocation on the ground floor. They were both watching the gang of workmen intently as they laboured at clearing the garden belonging to their flat, a sizeable section of land that was behind a stand of fir trees. Beyond the garden fence, through a gate, Norwood Lake could just be seen shimmering in the sun. It was only a small lake, little more than a large pond, but the space around it gave the local residents a place away from the city streets to jog, walk dogs, play ball and feed the ducks. It was an oasis in the concrete of London for birds to nest in, frogs to spawn in and small wild-life to forage in. Next to it were the school playing fields and a small children's playground, the swings and slide bright red against the bark-covered ground. The whistle of the tube train on its regular run to the City momentarily drowned the birdsong as it sped along its track on the other side of the lake, briefly over ground before diving back into the tunnels.

A tall man, blessed with a glorious overbite and a neck like a giraffe, Professor Oftentimes studied a plan laid out on the desk before him. It showed a line drawing of a garden pavilion, complete with picture window, French doors and small veranda. 'This'll be a fine solution to our space problem,' he said. 'Somewhere for you to study for school and to keep all your books and specimens.'

Jocelyn smiled at him. She was a studious ten year old with a passion for all creatures, great and small. She was fairly small herself for her age, with very curly blonde hair scraped back in a ribbon and a freckled face. She had the distracted, forgetful air of someone much older. Popular at school, even though she was quite bonkers about animals, the garden pavilion would also be a space she could share with her friends.

'At last it will mean that you'll be able to expand your laboratory too, Father. We're choc-a-bloc with veterinary implements, cages and medicines.'

'I leave most of it at the surgery on the ground

floor.' He protested. 'It's only the very special, most interesting cases that I bring up here.'

'Yes, and I love helping you when I'm allowed, but more space for me will still be good.'

Her father looked down affectionately at her.

'I know.' He hugged her.

Suddenly there was shouting from the garden below and one of the workmen barked out an order.

'Stop digging!'

The gang all gathered round, peering at something at the base of the shed.

'Come on!' Said Jocelyn and they both bolted out of the door and down the stairs, headed for the incident in the garden.

'There's something down there.' said Eric, the foreman, pointing down at the side of the shed. Professor Oftentimes and Jocelyn moved closer, the professor's scruffy pullover making him only slightly less well dressed than the labourers.

'It's a fox,' said the Professor. 'My goodness, it must have been living here some time from the look of it.'

'Oh! Father! We can't hurt it. What are we to do?' exclaimed Jocelyn. A look of hopeful craftiness filled her eyes. 'Guess what? We need a tagged wild animal for my year's school nature project. We've been talking to the Wildlife Trust and were thinking of a pigeon or a mouse if we were lucky. But a fox... now that would be something truly interesting. Please Father - we could watch where it goes. I know we have an electronic collar indoors.'

Professor Oftentimes hesitated. He looked at Jocelyn, then the hole, then at Jocelyn again, then at the assembled workmen, as if the answer to his dilemma could be found in any of their faces. He opened his mouth to speak and then shut it again. He bent down, smelled the musky, earthy smell of the fox's den and stood up.

Jocelyn held her breath. It felt like hours had passed. It was an outside chance.

Finally, the professor bent down again, gave a sort of snort and said, 'Jocelyn, go and get a sack, a net and an animal crate from the surgery.'

Knowing she had won, she ran as fast as she could to fulfill the errand, a huge smile breaking out over her face, red with excitement.

Becky Beaky, Jasper's pet pigeon, sat high up on the post of the washing line in the garden next door, surveying the proceedings around Jasper's home with alarm. She was typical of London pigeons, rather threadbare and mucky with one toe missing where she had caught it in a wire bird feeder while trying to steal peanuts. She daren't fly down to talk to him, so she woo-wooed loudly to let him know she was there giving him moral support.

Jocelyn arrived back at the shed in the time it might have taken an Olympic runner. They spread the net out across the entrance to Jasper's den, a rope threaded all the way around it so it could be closed in an instant.

'OK - you two men hold the ropes and don't let go. You open the door to the crate and hold the sack Jocelyn. Stand back everyone!' called Professor Oftentimes.

Jasper, realising he was in grave danger, had retreated to the back of his den where he could peer through a small hole in the wood at the bottom of the shed, like a frightened infant on a stormy night. Grateful for Becky's noisy presence nearby, he waited. Jasper knew he was excellent at waiting. He had once waited seven and a half hours for a miracle, before he was called away to inspect a particularly stunning dustbin. He could see Eric, hacking at the brambles and exposing the hole in the fence that he used to get to the lake at night. The man was facing the other way.

'If I could just make a run for it', thought Jasper, 'I might be able to slip through that hole and make it to the bushes. After all, I have all the natural instincts of a trickster – I'm a fox!'

Taking a deep breath, with a gulp, he made his break.

Pandemonium broke loose.

He could hear shouting. He felt the net close around him and snarled as he turned towards the men holding it, lashing out with his claws and teeth. He thrashed and flailed, he bit the net, but he couldn't escape. The next thing he knew was it all went dark as he was dropped into the sack and, still inside it, shoved into the crate. The door slammed shut. He lay panting in the bottom, tangled in the net and hot and stuffy in the sack. He was trying not to be afraid. After all, he was voted fox most likely to be hunted to extinction two years running and he was still here wasn't he? He could feel himself being carried and he heard the Woo-Woo of Becky come nearer as he felt himself being taken into the building.

'OK, put him down there,' said the Professor to the two men carrying the crate into the surgery. 'Thank you. You can get back to work now.'

The men did as they were bid and went back outside, full of the story they would tell their families when they got home.

'Now then young Jocelyn, before I fit the collar on our friend here, I'll re-configure the tracking so that you can access its GPS signal over the internet to follow where he goes.'

Jocelyn took the collar, grey plastic with a small box on the side of it, light and strong, and plugged a cable between it and the laptop computer. She looked at the bundle still writhing in the crate and felt an urge to stroke the poor thing and whisper some words of comfort, but thought that a human touch might just make him more jumpy.

'Right, let's calm this young fellow down so we can check him over. Then put a microchip in him so we can be sure he's our fox after he's been set free.' He took a syringe out of his bag and opened the crate.

The fox sighed and slumped, unconscious, onto the crate floor. They gently lifted him out and disentangled him from the net. Laying him on the table, Professor Oftentimes made sure the injection had worked well and he was properly asleep before he started to examine him and fit the collar.

Jasper was floating. He had Becky Beaky by his side, flapping. He tried to think, which he normally did stupendously well for he had all the instincts of a Doctor of Philosophy, or at least an assistant librarian.

'She's asked for you,' said Becky, 'she especially asked for you – by name! Woo -Woo.'

'Who? Who has asked for me?'

'The Countess of Tooting,' said Becky. 'Quickly, she's not going to last long.'

'Whoever she is, doesn't she know that I've been having an eventful time? I am not given to panic. Truth is I am remarkably calm, having all the instincts of a Shaolin Monk – or perhaps a marble statue, but everything has become quite strange.'

They entered a room. Lying on a velvet cushion was a large, champagne-coloured poodle with a bow in her very curly hair and freckles all over her aged snout, her body overhanging the cushion like an avalanche. Jasper introduced himself with a breathtakingly handsome bow.

'I know who you are,' said the Countess.

'I assumed you'd know,' said Jasper, 'I am one of a kind.'

The Countess sank back on her bed, coughing

feebly.

'I haven't got long. There is something very special I need you to promise to me before I die.'

Jasper thought she was being shockingly melodramatic – must have a fondness for the theatre.

'Relax,' he said, 'it's a scientific fact that hysteria causes freckles.'

'Becky, be a dear and pass me that box,' said the countess, indicating a small casket.

Becky flew and landed the box in front of the Countess of Tooting, just near enough for her to open it. Inside was a beautiful chain necklace, light as gossamer, fragile as a cobweb and silvery as the moon. It pooled in Jasper's paw as she dropped it there and laid her own over it.

'This necklace is my most precious possession. It bears the heritage of my long and distinguished pedigree and has magic properties that will only be released on my death. I beg you to take this and put it around the neck of a fairy trapped by a spell in a tree on Clapham Common, but not until the next full moon, which will also be the start of term. It's the only thing that will break the spell and I owe it to her to make sure she is freed. You'll know which tree because Becky will show you. The fairy's name is Miss Jocy Sometimes.'

Becky Woo-Wooed and tipped her head to one side knowingly.

'The Countess of Tooting was her show-dog long ago and Jocy loves the Countess like a granddaughter, or perhaps a second cousin twice removed. It was to save the Countess that she accepted the spell, cast on her by an angry Fox Hound, Gonzo Bane, because he came second to the Countess at the International Aristocrat Dog Show some time ago. The spell is hard to break because only a fox can carry the necklace. So she chose you.'

To Jasper it seemed like the perfect time to gloat shamelessly.

'It will be dangerous,' said the Countess. 'The dog walkers will soon know I have died and realise the necklace is unleashed. They are everywhere, in many guises, so you must take the utmost care. Don't let any strangers befriend you. Nobody tried to on your way here did they?'

'Hundreds, darling. I'm the sort of fox who attracts a crowd. But you can trust me with this task. It makes perfect sense. Nothing gets past Jasper Chap. But if I do this for you, what's in it for me?'

'I know you have no home and can't go back to your larder hole, so I have hidden five hundred Creds for you as soon as you get back from your mission.'

'*Five hundred Creds! Wow!*' thought Jasper. That's more than enough to buy a really comfortable den – and possibly a monkey.

'Go, quickly. I am fading fast and wish to be alone with my memories.'

'You're looking very poorly,' said Jasper with heart-breaking tact.

The Countess waved her paw weakly and gasped,

sounding like a horse with a nail in its hoof.

'Wear it round your neck to keep it safe. Your fur will hide it.'

They were dismissed. Leaving the room Jasper and Becky shot the Countess a last wave and they were on their way. The morning light, with all its promise and menace seemed a million miles away.

Having checked his collar, thinking that his fur would hide it, Jocelyn and Professor Oftentimes carefully carried the crate with the sleeping fox into the garden. They set it down next to the gate to the lake and propped the door open so that he could escape free when he woke up. There was a mangy looking pigeon perched on the fence making a bit of a racket as they crept away.

On the last day before the end of the summer holidays Jocelyn came home from the library with the 'Daily Bugle' newspaper for the professor, as she did every day. On the front page there were photos of a fox at the top of an Underground escalator. Jocelyn rushed to show her father.

Professor Oftentimes was watching the local evening news on the television when she ran into the room. There was a report about a fox being spotted going down an escalator to the trains below. Someone had even caught a video of it on their phone.

'Jocelyn, I think we'd better look where your fox has got to.'

They both went and sat at his desk in the corner.

'Well, I never,' said the Professor.

They looked at each other, then at the computer screen where the tracking software was showing a trail, then back at each other.

'How the Devil did he get to Clapham Common station?'

'And what on earth is he doing there?'

Down to Earth

Sue Wright

She looked across the headland to see two people standing face to face silhouetted against the sky. The evening light cast the image across the intervening cove and offered it to this drab little woman in a beige mac. It seemed as if the couple kissed before moving away but maybe that was her interpretation. She thought about how odd it was that those two people would never know that she had plucked them from the skyline and drawn them in. The two of them were in her memory now; she would not put them back.

She watched the sun's rays reach towards the horizon, all of her attention held as the clouds turned ever more brightly orange. Then she turned, taking the path that led homewards, but her thoughts contained the sunset. She placed her feet carefully, deliberately, as if to confirm her presence on the earth; her connection so fragile that it needed the affirmation of heel and toe upon the ground. Despite the muscles of her feet and legs proclaiming their existence, her mind continued to float. It rose and fell in rhythm with the movement of her body. Thoughts came and went, unattached to any particular meaning;

a word here, a picture there. The random drifting kept the reality of her life away.

At the first sign of her mind taking her in the direction of ordinary worries, not to mention her deepest fears and anxieties, she would run a nursery rhyme through in her head. Softly at first, the tune wove in and out of other vague thoughts until it found its way out of her mouth as a sound. It started as a breathy whisper that flew upwards on the wind. It became a low murmur; wordless mumbling which lilted into babbling. Up and down and over and over, a simple little melody that increased in volume until she felt comforted by its familiarity. Then words came, bouncing along with her steps.

It took effort to keep the tedium of her lonely life at bay. Her fists were pushed hard inside her pockets and she maintained a deep frown while she sang. Her feet trod harder with each beat of the rhythm and jarred her knees. She tried to ignore the pain in her joints but it slowed her down. She stopped a moment and turned to look back at the emptiness of the cliff top path where she had stood to watch the sunset. A gust of wind from the sea hit her and she shivered, so that a reminder of her cold, empty bedsit caught her unawares.

As she trudged towards home, both the song and the will to sing it had left her. Only dullness remained. She didn't notice that a lace in one of her boots slipped a little further undone with each step until it caught beneath the sole of her other foot and tripped her up. She fell heavily forward, landing on her pained knees and scraping her palms and elbows. She sat for a while, winded and forlorn, looking down at the mud on her charity shop mac, and began to cry.

UGLY AS SIN *and other clichés*

Not My Cup of Tea

Dawn Morgan

I had not seen him before at the coffee house. A wisp of a man, he bent his head backwards on his long neck like a leek in a winter garden, to keep his spectacles on his nose. A rough wind blew past him as he pushed open the door, and I swear I saw his periwig go adrift by several inches in his struggle to enter the place. With one arm on the door and the other around a bundle of books, he had no free hand to encourage the furry beast back onto his poll. Only after he had shuffled to a table and laid his volumes in a pile, did he scurry his wayward hairpiece into a sober position on his crown.

But I had seen the pale hair that lay in greasy stripes beneath: a young man's hair, despite his eyeglasses. And I confess that this sly sighting gave me a sense of advantage. So, I wore a saucy look as I sauntered over to him.

'What will you have, sir?' I said, leaning forward to brush the table.

He looked up, clearly alarmed at the sight of me, or my saucy expression.

'Will you take coffee?' I asked, curling my lips. 'Or chocolate, for warmth?'

He searched past me as if in need of help, fixing his eyes on a comradely group at the next table. One of those gentlemen – Mr Pepys – winked at me, before raising his cup in greeting to the stranger.

'A fair day,' said Mr Pepys, nodding with a certainty that bolstered his words.

'Ah… yes,' said our young guest, stabbing a glance towards the windows, which squealed to the wind's tune and cast the sky's pallor into the room. He seemed to consider his reply for a careful moment. 'A fair day,' he said at last.

Pepys gave a genial smile and returned to his comrades.

'There is some fine debate to be had with that gentleman,' he said. 'Most agreeable.'

The boy flushed amid the billow of laughter. I gave Mr Pepys a tart look.

'If all were so agreeable, I should call myself fortunate,' I said. 'But I'll never find my fortune here, I think.'

'I fear you won't,' said Mr Pepys. 'Although you raise your prices as often as our spirits. Try the China drink,' he said to the boy. 'It is a fine brew. I drank it for the first time this year and I can vouch for its flavour.'

'Yes, why not take a cup of China tea?' I offered. 'Our house will treat you, for your first visit.'

I stole a glance at my mother at the counter, who would skin me for such licence.

He cleared his throat. 'Thank you,' he said. 'That

is… yes, thank you.'

'They say it refreshes the spirits,' I told him, leaning down to speak more softly. 'Gives a sharpness to the mind.'

'Well,' he said, looking up at me, grey eyes under the glass. 'I will try it indeed.'

'Makes your piss run brown, though,' called Mr Pepys, blowing up a fresh gale of laughter. 'Dark as a China river.'

'None of the flash talk if you please,' I said, without rancour. 'Take no notice,' I added to the boy. 'He has not pissed since he arrived.'

Then I took his startled look back to the counter, enjoying the warmth of it as I fetched his first cup of tea.

I made sure to keep my eyes on the boy as I went about my work, and I swear that at six o'clock he had drunk no more tea, nor any other beverage, nor spoken to any gentleman, but he had squinted all the afternoon over his books, so I was perplexed at it and resolved to learn his business. My chance came when my mother took to chiding a serving girl for sluttishness and was much occupied by the labour.

'Would you take more tea?' I asked him.

'Eh?' he answered, looking up distractedly, his spectacles going awry.

I smiled. 'Shall I bring you another cup, for a penny? Or would coffee sweeten your toils?'

He shook his head. 'No, thank you.' Then he stooped again over his book, as if his shoulder would bid me leave him be.

I was put out by this and determined to stir him.

'But sir,' I said, touching the purse that hung at my belt, jangling it a little so that the coins inside moved tunefully.

'I fear you may fall sick from warmth and dryness in this house unless you take more refreshment.'

He took my point and extracted a penny from his own purse, his cheeks becoming rosier.

'I will take more tea,' he said, placing the penny in my outstretched palm. 'Thank you.'

'A pleasure, sir,' I answered, glancing at the open book before him. I bent to spy on it more closely, but could make out only a dozen words before he placed his hand across the page.

'Forgive me,' I said, 'I have a great curiosity to know what you are about.'

'I study,' he said.

Although I waited for more, none was offered. I pressed him further. 'Do you study for pleasure, or advancement?'

'For both,' he answered.

'And why in such a raucous place as this?'

I looked around at the many gentlemen who sat or stood about the room, conversing or conducting their business. He muttered some words about his attic, which he said was in a sad pickle on account of the roof, but he spoke very reluctantly.

'Well, with luck a warm draft will give you strength for discourse,' I said, taking his penny.

I went to fetch his tea from the barrel and left him to his labours.

Our house being very full and merry that evening, it was near seven o'clock before I had my chance to vex him further. On approaching him, I saw that his cup stood untouched, and I wondered at it, since he had parted with his penny so charily.

'Do you not like it, sir?' I asked, picking up the cup and seeing my own features swimming on the dark surface.

He gave an uneasy laugh, 'It was somewhat gloomy in flavour,' he admitted.

'Then you liked the first, but not the second?'

He remained silent and had such a glum look in his own face that I laughed aloud, a merry bark that my mother heard across the room.

'Bess, what are you twittering about there?' she shouted.

'I am taking this gentleman's order for China tea,' I called back.

The boy looked alarmed at that, but I winked at him.

'Do not worry,' I said, 'I would not make you more gloomy.'

I was rewarded with a most pleasant smile, and a puckering around his eyes that brought a sweet light to them, so I walked away quite giddy and bumped into three gentlemen on my way to the counter.

As soon as I was able, I made it my business to taste the China tea, that I had never drunk before.

The boy's cup being stale, I went to the barrel, where I had poured the day's allowance of boiled tea that morning, before the excise man came to assess us on the commodity. I dipped in a ladle and drew some liquid into a pan, which I took to the fire and heated — as was our usual practice — then I tipped the hot liquid into a cup.

I put my lips to the brim and drank a good swig of the brown potion. Then I threw the rest of it into the drain and walked directly to the lad's table.

'You may keep your penny, sir,' I told him, placing a coin by his elbow. 'It is foul stuff indeed.'

You Only Live Once

Sue Wright

Veronica had already been through security and was standing there in her socks, gathering her belongings and shoving them back into her carry-on bag when the alarm went off. She stood perfectly still, waiting for someone to know what to do. Her hands, poised in imminent movement reminded her of playing statues as a child. She'd always felt anxious in that frozen moment, where time stopped.

The passengers were herded, pushed and scurried around the local airport and eventually loaded onto a different flight going south. Their luggage remained on the tarmac. Although it was a short flight, when they landed at Heathrow they were late, so late that she had to run to catch the plane that was to carry her to her big adventure.

By the time she caught her breath again, she was seated, her hand luggage stowed above her, shoes kicked off and handbag beneath the seat in front. She pulled her knees up so that her socked feet were curled around the front edge of the seat and hugged herself. 'You only live once' they had told her, and here she was, finally on her way, her excitement tinged with nerves.

Seated directly behind her was a dull-looking middle aged man, the kind of man that goes through life largely unnoticed, with a face that seldom smiles. His fingers were clasped across the buckle of his seatbelt, his thumbs nervously circling each other. He bit the inside of one cheek and stared at the small screen in front of him, trying to ignore the clunk of overhead lockers being firmly shut and the mutterings of late comers as they found their seats. The rapid strides and clipped voices of the cabin crew going about their business grated on him. He had never liked flying much.

As the plane began its roll towards the runway, he held his breath and stared straight ahead. The reflection of his profile in the window glass shuddered as the engines revved up to their full crescendo for take-off, and the landscape sped by. When the plane lifted, and the familiar shapes of London shrank into minutiae far below, his destiny was well and truly forged. The muscles of his neck and shoulders tightened a fraction more and his stomach clenched. He ordered a large whisky.

The plane was a mile high before Veronica remembered that her luggage was not on the flight. How would she manage with no belongings in a strange country, in a new job where she knew no-one? She would have no money until her first pay cheque. A bubble of fear rose from the depths of her stomach into the back of her throat, but she swallowed it down. A stewardess leaned towards her and she sat up, glad to be distracted. After a glass of wine, she felt better and found that she was hungry too and her curry was surprisingly good. What the hell, she'd worry about it when she got there.

The man behind her chose the vegetarian option. He removed the foil from the main course and winced at the steamy smell. He ate methodically, steadily; working his way around the tray in a clockwise direction, then wiping his mouth and letting his attention rove around the cabin. Behind him, an American woman was speaking with strident cheerfulness to her neighbour, a young man across the aisle was engrossed in his phone, two thumbs flicking in constant movement over a brightly coloured game, and there was an intermittent glimpse of a bald head and a hairy ear between two seats.

He amused himself for as long as he could but eventually the atmosphere started to close in on him. Feeling trapped was a familiar state for him. Keep your head down. Don't rock the boat. Do as you are told. Work, work, work and more work. Make sure you do it right. Get on with it. Work late. Obey the rules. That is, until the day he chose not to.

It had only taken the movement of a finger to move the money from where it belonged into his own account, so easily, and he had moved it back and forth more than once to confirm how easy it would be. Such a small amount in the grand scheme of things, they wouldn't miss it - surely? And then, after one final transaction, he had walked out of the office in the middle of the afternoon without looking back. He simply did not care anymore.

Now, that was an unaccustomed feeling that he could not remember ever having felt before. He had walked the length of Piccadilly twice before plucking up the courage to order afternoon tea in Fortnum and Mason. He had sat in a corner, pretending to belong, pouring tea from a silver tea pot, eating exquisite sandwiches and tasting the most wonderful cakes he had ever eaten. He licked the last of the sugar from his lips as he paid the bill, an astonishing amount of money.

At the end of what he told himself had been a very reasonable spree, he was determined not to waste another moment of his new found freedom. He would book himself a well-deserved holiday, a long one, perhaps a trip across the Atlantic. However, it had proved more difficult than he thought to break a lifetime habit of thrift. When it came to it, he hadn't been able to bring himself to waste money on a first class ticket. Only now he was beginning to regret his parsimony.

A wailing child at the other end of the plane assaulted his ears and brought him back to the present. He looked up to see Veronica edge her way around her neighbours to get to the loo. He watched her as she waited outside the occupied cubicle, shifting her weight from one foot to the other, staring at the floor. She bent down to pull up her socks, then stood up and folded her arms. He wondered how it was that young people always managed to look so carefree. When she emerged and saw him watching her he looked away immediately.

On the way back to her seat, she stole another glance in his direction. She thought he looked worried and entertained herself for a while by inventing a life for him. Perhaps he was lonely, perhaps he had a wife that died, no, it was more likely he was divorced she decided. Definitely no children. He didn't look like anyone's Dad. Mind you, you could never really tell. She named him Mr Smith. She eased herself into her seat and leaned back picturing his tiny bedsit, the calendar on the wall by the sink, the threadbare sofa with unmatched cushions in shades of grey.

Behind her, Mr Smith adjusted his screen that was now at an odd angle and reached for the earbuds in his the pocket in front of him. He knocked back the last of his whisky and settled down to James Bond. After a while he drifted in and out of sleep so that the film and his dreams merged. One moment he was involved in a wild car chase, the next he was looking down the barrel of a gun or being uncharacteristically resourceful when faced with danger.

As it happened, Veronica's screen was showing the same film although she wasn't paying much attention to it. Eventually her mind settled and she too slept. It was an uneventful night.

When the lights came up they both woke to the murmur of awakening passengers that rippled along the length of the plane. A series of indecipherable announcements accompanied the watery coffee and rubbery scrambled egg.

When the plane touched down, Veronica and Mr Smith extricated themselves from their cramped positions and stood eye to eye in the narrow aisle. She was surprised that he was not much taller than she was and decided that perhaps he looked fatherly after all.

After a few wrong turns, Veronica eventually found her way to the information desk, only to see that Mr Smith was there already. When she leaned on the counter beside him, he nodded politely and gestured for her to go first. She thanked him with a nod and launched into the sorry tale about the left behind luggage. The more her voice rose, the more his own concerns diminished. She turned angrily away from the desk, and he timidly offered to buy her a coffee. She accepted, rather ungraciously, but by the end of the second cup she had calmed down and was able to thank him properly for his kindness. Mr Smith, feeling reckless for the second time in his life leaned towards her.

'Hold out your hand.'

Veronica looked at him doubtfully.

'Hold out your hand.'

She did so and he placed a large wad of notes on her palm and closed her fingers over the top. She looked down in disbelief at the vast amount of money he had given her.

Mr Smith was enjoying his newfound boldness and

deciding that he knew better than the bank how investments should be spent. What was the point of hoarding for hoarding's sake? This poor girl needed help and he had the wherewithal to do it. Surely the universe had given him this opportunity to do a good deed with the bank's money. The fact that he was also getting one over on his old employer was a bonus.

He felt like a new man and insisted on helping her set off on her big adventure. After all, you only live once. He saw her into a taxi and waved goodbye. Feeling inordinately pleased with himself, he hailed another for himself, enjoying the novelty of having it to himself. The yellow cab pulled away and Mr Smith settled back with a sigh. Only the driver noticed the police car tailing them.

UGLY AS SIN *and other clichés*

Teacher's Pet

Dawn Wyndham

'The cat sat on the mat.'

In large chalk script on the black board at the front of the class, the phrase stood guard while the kids at their desks chanted it by rote. They were in their first year. Small and new; boys and girls. In two/two time they read the words out loud, face to the front, each voice lost in the mix of high and low, loud and soft. It could have been a song; it had a lilt to it that made them sound like a choir.

She stood with her back to the board, her green eyes shut as, in her mind's eye, she was back in last night. She had run to his side. His strong grip on her neck, her moan as he thrust his hard self in her. How she did want him. She had no choice. She was his. What Tom wants, Tom gets. It was his right. It was his need. There was not a thing he could do to stop it, no more than she could stop a need of her own. It was meant to be.

She shook the thought off and brought her gaze back to the class. Head high, with a sway of her back and a swing of her hips she took a walk round the room. Just last week they had all come here for their first day at school, wide-eyed and fresh. The new school year told a tale of hope. She liked them when they were this young, their minds a blank sheet. They did not know what they did not know and they did not care. So much to learn, they had a thirst to soak up each fact like a sponge. She was proud that she was here with them, that she was a rare treat to these Babes in the Wood, a help to drown the fear of their first step on the long road that will lead, at the end, to the loss of their youth.

A bell rang. Time to close the class. One by one the kids went out in a line. It was the end of the school day. Free to go at last, with a shriek and a laugh at the chance to make some noise and not be told what it should be, they made a bolt for the door.

The room was a void now they were gone. The sun shone gold rays through the panes of glass to light the floor. She swept one last look between the desks. Time to go. With a deep sigh and a stretch she left the room through the door they had fled by.

She knew she was great to watch. She took long strides with a slow grace and wove through the streets at her own pace. Like an old friend, she knew this route well. She took it each day to the school and back just so she could be in the class. They were all so dear to her! The way they felt for her, the pure way they gave her their own love back and, with a stroke, held her close.

Her guts made a noise. She had to eat. She thought back to the meal she ate last night. Fish, white fish;

best of all, with no bones. She could catch a mouse.

She was home. Just a step through the French door.

She knew that soon, Tom would be back.

She sat on the mat.

Written entirely in words of one syllable.

UGLY AS SIN *and other clichés*

Step by Step

Sue Wright

The front door of an ordinary semi-detached house, in an ordinary suburban street, opens. A man standing in the hallway hesitates, looks back over his shoulder into the house before stepping outside, pulling the door firmly shut behind him. He pushes against it twice and tries the handle twice. Posting a key though the letterbox, he assures himself that there is no access to what the house contains. His exit is interrupted briefly at the gate which he wedges shut with one of its own broken slats. Shaking his head, he continues along the pavement without looking back.

His pace is slow but steady. He has small feet for a man of his height, shod in well-polished brogue shoes. These are well past their best, a fact that the polish hasn't quite managed to disguise. He is slightly pigeon toed which makes each step he takes appear excessively precise.

Rather at odds with his choice of footwear, he is wearing an old pair of trousers spattered down one leg with a dark coloured spillage and frayed at the hem. They are worn so thin that the threadbare left leg exposes a glimpse of bony knee with each alternate step he takes. He thrusts his hands deeper into the pockets of his thin denim jacket and leans forward into the wind. His head sinks down and he hunches his shoulders as if enduring an onslaught to the back of his neck. His hair although long, is thin on top and does not afford him much protection.

A small red car pulls up alongside him and the woman driver calls across.

'Hey…Len…..?'

He doesn't look up and she watches him whilst she eases the car forward at walking pace. She is eye level with his legs.

'Is June at home? I wanted to arrange a get together. Are you OK? Is that blood on your leg?'

He lifts an arm as if to protect himself and turns his head away from her. He takes a sharp left turn down an alleyway where the car can't follow. She drives on, shaking her head.

He grits his teeth and speeds up his pace, unaware that he is muttering aloud. 'Silly cow……' although it isn't clear to whom he refers. He starts to count. '*One, two, three, four, five six, seven*' and back to one again; over and over. The counting fills his mind with soothing regularity. In his pocket he turns a penknife over and over in his hand in time with his steps.

He is beyond the houses now and walking on the grass verge of a dual carriageway. He abandons his count and lets the sound of each passing vehicle collide with his eardrums as it passes. He stands still for a moment with his eyes closed, relishing the full-blast oomph of a speeding sports car. He compares its passing with the deep rumble of a heavily laden tractor and trailer which reverberates lower down in his body. As each vehicle passes, he experiences them differently and listens for the repeated whine of tyres on tarmac and the jarring alteration in tone as each one hits a small pot hole.

In sight of the suspension bridge, he sits down abruptly and removes his shoes. He peels off each sock, places them carefully inside each shoe and puts the shoes together by a lamp post, patting them gently like an old friend. He flexes his toes and grunts as he pulls himself to his feet once more. Spotting an old cigarette packet, he stares at it a moment before picking it up. He sees how muddy it is on one side, turns it over and notices how the colour has faded but the words 'smoking kills' can still be read. He looks at his own stained fingers holding the packet and smiles without humour. He takes off his wedding ring and places it inside the packet before letting it drop. Perhaps he hopes that one day someone will be surprised to discover it there; or perhaps his thoughts are entirely to do with letting go. He raises his head and creases his forehead. His eyes gauge the distance he has yet to walk to reach his destination. Realising that he has been holding his breath, he lets out a single sigh.

Now, he walks more cautiously, and feels the difference between a patch of grass and a muddy puddle on the soles of his feet. The muscles do not contract against the cold and he wonders if his body and brain are still connected. Inside his pockets, he digs his thumbnails into his forefingers and feels nothing. Pulling his hands out, he scrutinises them, curls the fingers inwards, and observes the palm lines that crumple into deeper creases. Perhaps his fate was written there all along, his actions, reactions and behaviours predetermined; but here is no longer any meaning for him in what he has experienced or what he has done or why he may have done what he did. There is only walking.

Just as he reaches the bridge, the sun sends a brief shaft of light directly onto the water beneath, highlighting a group of small boats and the white rim of their colliding wake. He stops to lean on the rail and contemplate the panorama before him. He watches the darkening of the walls of the factory on the far bank as the sun resumes its place behind the cloud. There is an almost imperceptible mist, which feels pleasant on his face and has the effect of softening the edges of everything within his sight. In the distance he wonders exactly where the sea meets the sky, both above and below are grey today, there is no horizon to be clearly seen.

His eyes roam slowly from side to side, and his head tilts as he catches sight of the row of small cottages, one of which is his home. He cannot quite see the broken gate from this distance. He sighs once more and removes his jacket. He feels in the pocket, draws out a few coins and the penknife. He drops them one by one over the railing and watches them fall. It is a long while before they hit the water. He doesn't hear any of them make a splash.

He is ready now. He glances in both directions along the road which is momentarily clear of cars. He climbs onto the railing and levers himself over to the other side. He is standing on a narrow ledge, with his toes bending down towards the water. His arms are stretched, crucifixion-wise as his hands clasp the top rail behind him. He leans his body forward a little, still holding onto the rail. He can see the movement of the waves on the water far below.

Behind him he senses a car going past, and another, and another. He hears a screech of brakes and voices. They are only a few yards away but seem to him as if they come from another world. He cannot distinguish meaningful words; he only hears the rapid urgency of their interchange. He doesn't know if they are men or women, he doesn't care what they do or say. He vaguely registers a pitter-patter sound, undefined to him; perhaps it is raindrops or hailstones. It is in fact the footsteps of the person now standing a yard or so away from him. A woman standing there is mouthing words at him. He hears sounds but is unable to ascribe any meaning to them. He looks sideways at her, fascinated by the movement of her mouth, the occasional exposure of her small white teeth. She gesticulates, a pleading gesture and frowns a little.

He leans a little further forward, sliding his arms

closer together behind him. The woman makes a sharp intake of breath no louder than the wind already in his ears. He releases one arm to push back the hair from his eyes. There is no way back now. The sound of a distant siren is experienced in his inner ear as a soaring note of extraordinarily piercing beauty to accompany his fall. It is the last thing he hears.

If at First You Don't Succeed

Dawn Wyndham

That's it. Enough! I'm giving up smoking.

Day 1:

Shit.

Day 1 again - only the next day:

Have tried to kill eldest daughter twice. Have nailed dog's feet to the floor. Decide against clearing up dishes as always have cigarette when done. Same for bathroom. Am suddenly thinking this has upside. Eating dried fruit, apricots, pears, and brown things that look like squished earwigs, which remind me of tobacco, which remind me of cigarettes. Walk into garden. Watch neighbour light a cigarette; look at him pityingly. Eat leftover beans from last night - that'll show them. Walk by computer and wave occasionally. Can't sit and write or surf yet as this has been main smoking area. It's about four o' clock now; I could have just one, I could have just one, I could have just one.

That's Mr. Nicotine. He lives with me; 'he' could be a 'she', but frankly, right now, I don't fucking care. Decide to play fantasy game on PC. Spend next three hours fighting anything I meet so game hero can save world.

World doomed in my opinion.

Day 2, morning:

Woke up two hours earlier than usual. Great; two extra hours of fencing practice with the British American Tobacco Company and spawn. Seriously considering finding some hallucinogens as never had desire for nicotine during a really good walk through a wall. Woke up six times during night to pee because I drank four gallons of water 'to assist my system flush poison.' Am feeling unusually testy as result of lack of sleep and deep-seated oral fixation fantasies. Decide to either kill, or have sex with postman when post arrives. Probably both.

Day 2, afternoon:

Clean cupboards. Nothing new in the post. Did all laundry out of necessity - body of dead postman would not fit in dryer otherwise. Decide to walk dog. Meet neighbour who asks if post has come yet. He is smoking a cigarette. I tell him 'no' out of spite.

Day 3, morning:

Go through dead man's post bag; keep catalogues for joyous clothes shopping. Feed rest down waste disposal unit.

Day 3, afternoon:

Call waste disposal unit repair company.

Day 4:

Receive visitor. Police, looking for missing postman, received anonymous tip from waste disposal repair person. Make coffee and offer fat-free biscuits and dried fruit. Arrange dried fruit to make smiley faces on plate. Police officer asks if I mind if he smokes. Burst into tears.

Confess.

Day 272:

Sentenced to life for murder of postal employee.

Day 278:

Beaten by seven large women in prison for having no cigarettes to trade. Able to sing better now I've been nearly strangled; make up prison blues songs.

Day 452:

Receive divorce papers: husband marrying tobacco heiress. Cell-mate offers to have ex-husband beaten up. Wants twelve cartons of cigarettes and one pair Doc Marten boots. Decide husband will live as price too steep.

Day 458:

Secure two cartons of cigarettes for payment to cell-mate to have defence lawyer beaten up. Feel better.

Day 491:

Served last meal. Vicar asks if anything wanted in last moments. Think back to how good cigarette after meals used to be. Request one last smoke. Minister reluctant, no smoking in death cell, but sneaks one in. Sit back, relax, smoke. Ahhhhh. Feel slightly dizzy, giddy, euphoric. Prison guard enters cell excitedly; Queen issues full pardon due to new crimes statute: allows for defence appeal of insanity by reason of severe nicotine withdrawal.

Day 1:

Shit.

'Mum, Mu-um, MUMMY!'

'Oh!' Blink, blink.

Awakened from nightmare by the children rushing into the bedroom and leaping onto the bed. How can they be so lively this early in the morning? I've got two. Both girls. Phoebe, 8 and Tina, 6. They are delightful replicas of their Dad and me. I stretch and sigh, then give them both a 'Good morning' hug.

Time to get up.

It's a school day.

Better check the dryer.

First performed as a monologue by Harriet Thorpe in a selection of plays written for Zoom broadcast https://gauntandson.com/five-4-five

Sea Change

Sue Wright

The sound of the wind brushing the grass was like a half remembered sigh. He closed his eyes but the owner of the sigh would not come to him, not now. He breathed out, only then aware of how long he had held his breath to listen for the past. He breathed in the present moment, deeply; rose to his feet, brushed the twigs and leaves off the back of his thighs and stood for a while, his rucksack dangling from one hand. He looked out over the sea, feeling the alternating warmth and cold on his face as the clouds scuttled across the sun. He shouldered his rucksack a little awkwardly, the pain in his neck jabbed a reminder to him to be careful of it. He turned his head slowly from side to side, as far as the limit of its movement. He walked on at a comfortable pace, sidestepping ruts and avoiding puddles. The rhythm of his stride was regular and the pain in his neck gradually subsided. He had already been walking for more than a month. Step after step, no turning back. Walking was his life now, just walking. Walking erased things.

There were voices up ahead, random chunks of

conversation that were not meant for his ears but nevertheless entered his mind.

'Whose fault was it?'

'Why on earth…'

'They should never have..'

'Really?'

'Really.'

He shivered. The rise and fall of their conversation, the cutting across each other, reminiscent of a past he could no longer recall, a long forgotten interaction perhaps. He hit the heel of his hand to his head as if to force the memories that would not come. The women who owned the voices looked sideways at him as they walked past in silence. When they picked up their conversation again, their small dog doubled back and began yapping at his ankles. He was unaccountably rattled and stumbled sideways which didn't deter the dog and he raised his arms in a gesture of defeat while the women watched. Then one of the women strode back towards him, scooped the dog up under one arm, nodded towards him and went back to her friend. He shook his head and rubbed his neck.

The flow of his walking had been disturbed. He looked at his watch. If he got a move on, he could make his next overnight stop before night fall. He had decided to treat himself to a B&B rather than camp out. It was time to have a proper shower and tidy up a bit, maybe wash a few things before carrying on. He turned away from the sea taking a narrow path up and over the cliff. He liked the different feel of tarmac beneath his feet after all the miles of uneven pathways. The signal on his phone was variable and the map was difficult to see, so when he finally reached his destination, it was dark.

He rang the bell and waited a few moments, listening to footsteps clip clopping along the tiled hallway. The frosted glass showed him a flash of bright yellow just before the door creaked open. He lowered his gaze to meet his hostess' welcoming smile, she barely came up to his shoulders. Her age was difficult to judge but her face bore the lines of many decades. He smiled at the bright sunflower brooch pinned to her cardigan and followed her down the hallway into the kitchen. There was a large well-scrubbed table in the centre of the room with a selection of mismatched chairs. One of them had had its back removed and laid on the floor beside it, one had no seat at all, just the frame where it had once been, but the rest looked as if they would just about hold a person. She indicated that he should sit down; he chose the least ancient looking chair and gingerly rested his elbows on the table itself. A vase of flowers at its centre wobbled and a few yellow petals fluttered loose and fell.

The old lady busied herself to and fro from cupboard to kettle to table and furnished him eventually with a cup of tea in a cracked mug. She didn't offer him milk but pushed a cut glass sugar bowl with a silver spoon across the table towards him.

The next five minutes were occupied with soothing platitudes about the weather and pleasantries about the season as a whole until they both lost interest and fell into silence. He sipped his tea noisily and after some minutes of this, she spoke.

'If you're walking eight miles a day it will take you a hundred days.'

He blinked at her.

'One end of Wales to the other, the coast path.'

He shook his head slowly before replying.

'There is no end for me, I'll keep going.'

'Oh, but there's always an end.'

'I doubt it.'

'You will know it when you reach it.'

'I don't think so.'

She tilted her head a little by way of disagreement and offered to show him to his room. Gratefully, he picked up his rucksack and walked up two flights of stairs to the tiny attic room that was his for the night. An even tinier room with a shower, toilet and miniscule washbasin was two steps away on the opposite side of the landing. Neither room had a door. If they had, they would have got in each other's way while opening or closing. Surprisingly, the shower turned out to be hot and vigorous, and the towel was large and thick. With the accumulated grime of the last few days scrubbed away, every single item of his clothing washed and draped on a radiator in the bedroom, he lay on the bed wearing only the towel. With his hands behind his head, ankles crossed one over the other he stared up at the night sky through the Velux window above him. The window was very slightly ajar and every time the wind blew it creaked a little. He found it soothing, reminding him of something but he couldn't remember what, and when sleep overtook him, it didn't matter.

It was not yet daylight when he woke to a strange sound coming from outside, a drone that rattled on and on then faded as it moved away into the distance when a sudden faint whistle told him it was probably a train. He lay there wakeful, listening as the sounds of the day crept up on him. There was traffic too, the stop and go of vehicles approaching and negotiating a bend. There was an occasional blast of music from an open car window. As time went on he heard voices, chattering children heading for school, irritable parents in a hurry. When he caught the smell of burnt toast, he thought it was time he got up and went to see what the old lady would offer him for breakfast.

He pulled on a slightly damp pair of jeans and a creased T-shirt and went downstairs in his bare feet. The smell of frying bacon made him realise how hungry he was but also prompted a sudden, unaccountable sadness. He frowned and swallowed, rubbing his hand over his neck where the scar was. The old lady put a plate of food in front of him with a large mug of coffee. There was bacon, sausages, eggs, tomatoes and unburnt toast, (presumably a second attempt).

She sat down opposite him with her own cup and saucer.

'No mushrooms, no beans, am I right?'

He looked across and she smiled as she answered his unasked question.

'I always know what people need my dear. I have the gift.'

'You do?'

'Show me your palm.'

He put down his fork and leaned his arm across the table. She peered intently for some time before releasing his hand back to its task of eating breakfast. She said nothing until he had finished and was cupping his hands around the mug of coffee.

'Do you want to know what I can tell you?'

'Why not?'

'There are many reasons why not but you must tell me if you do want to hear what I have to say.'

'Ok then, tell me.'

'Your life has taken a turn.'

He raised an eyebrow.

'Yes, yes, everything you thought would be so for ever is no longer so. Much has been lost.'

'Like what?'

She looked straight at him, as if she could see beyond the back of his eyes and into his mind. She hesitated before speaking again.

'I was wrong, it is hidden, not lost.'

'What is?'

'What you are walking for, what you need to find

222

and why you don't want to find it.'

'You're talking in riddles now.'

'Perhaps. But you are not quite ready for the truth.'
He smiled at her.

'You are very kind but I have been told that it is
very unlikely that anything will come back to me.'

'Not impossible.'

'There was an accident of some kind. I have no
recollection of it. Dissociative Amnesia apparently.'

'It will come back to you when you are ready to
know it.'

'What will?'

'What you have hidden from yourself.'
He frowned.

'There are clues all around you, should you care to
pay attention.'

'Like what?'

'Colours, sounds, smells. They will lead you.'
She patted him on the wrist.

'Never mind. Like I say, when you are ready your
body will know. Then you will take three deliberate
breaths and it will come back to you.'

She said no more, but he was bothered by it.

He got up from the table, retrieved his belongings,
thanked her, paid, and left. At the gate he turned to
look back. She was waving at him through the
window, still adorned with her yellow brooch. He
lifted an arm in reply and set off towards the beach.
He deviated from the straight downward path in
favour of the walk along the ridge. The undergrowth

was up above his head, and in places he needed to push aside the brambles in order to get past. And then he rounded a bend and the sea was before him. He was surprised at the sharpness of the view. He seemed to know that he had seen it when it had been hot and bright, with a heat haze across the water so you could barely make out the opposite shore, unlike today. The breeze was cool on his face. If he had been here before, when was it? How many summers ago?

A butterfly alighted on his arm, white and beautiful. He watched as it flexed its wings and lifted into the air to be joined by another. 'Like people' he thought, they circle around each other for a while before heading in different directions. He walked on, watching his footing on the path and when he reached a recently gravelled section he looked up again. There was an inlet ahead of him so that the path veered inland to avoid it and he looked towards the distinctive rock formation of the limestone cliff. The honey coloured blocks reminded him of houses in the Cotswolds. He wondered whether he had ever been there and if so when. It seemed that the new path had been made several metres inland from the old one, due to the on-going erosion of the cliff. He could see where it had fallen away, revealing a considerable overhang.

Just then, he heard the honking of a dozen Canada geese flying overhead in formation. He bent back to look up at them, shielding his eyes from the sun. They swooped around the bay and flew straight over his head. The weight of his rucksack as he leaned back to see them better pulled him off balance and he fell onto his back. The grassy slope was steep and he slithered for some way before coming to a halt. His heart was beating fast and he tried to calm his breathing. He had already taken three slow deliberate breaths before he remembered the old woman's words. Too late, the breath sheered through the barrier to his memory and he ventured inside. There he found his wife, still alive, an image in his mind, smiling. Her yellow cotton dress fluttered about her knees. Her feet were planted firmly due to the gentle creaking movement of the boat while her little Shih Tzu ran figures of eight around her ankles. He smiled back at her until the image faded.

Within seconds, the missing pieces of the past bounded out and stabbed him through his already broken heart. It had been here, on this beach. They had sat with their picnic, enjoying the glint of the sun on the water. There had been a deep groan, a breaking away, an entire section of the cliff had engulfed them both, suddenly and without mercy. He had been badly injured and she never regained consciousness.

They said he was in shock, not to worry, that his life would come back to him soon. And now it had hit him with a vengeance. The pain of loss that had been too much to bear at the time now racked his body. The grief his mind had been avoiding, shuddered though him in waves as he lay there. It took some time, but eventually the fear and denial that had clogged his mind and his heart were scraped away. When he came to himself enough to think about what he now felt, he was surprised to discover that he was enveloped in a bittersweet cloak of pain and love that felt real and solid and warm. He felt alive as he sat up and faced the sea, dug his heels in and pushed himself back to higher ground. He remained there for some time, just listening to the soothing hush of the sea. And then, faintly, he could hear her sigh in his ear, feel her love in his heart, softly caressing his soul as he rose to his feet and walked. Walking brought things into focus.

Labour of Love

Dawn Morgan

'It is your scent, ma'am,' I said.

Her eyes remained as cool as violets under the dew, but her pink mouth crinkled at the corners, and she raised her teacup to mask the twitching of her lips.

'That is to say... forgive me,' I said, clearing my throat. 'It is your capacity to scent the leaves, ma'am, and thereby determine any improper substances within them, that is your best defence against the tea's adulteration.'

'Indeed?' answered Miss Blackwell. 'And you are not?'

I sat oblique from her in silence, stunned as a sheep that has been knocked on the head before slaughter.

'I had hoped to look to you for such protection,' she continued, 'since you are an expert in these matters.'

She followed her words with a mouthful of scalding Souchong, that was surely too hot to drink, and showed no squeamishness as the fiery brew assaulted her mouth, or when it reached her white throat. As the liquid began to descend, it made a glutinous sound, which rose to a wet crescendo in passing her Adam's apple.

'I shall protect you!' I said, sitting higher in my seat.

Immediately, I wanted to draw back my words. I emitted a sucking sound – not unlike the slurping of tea as practiced by my less genteel customers, when they come to sample the latest leaves in the parlour of my shop. This sound made a circuit of the room, overtaking the vibrations of the young lady's digestion, and was punctuated by a noise from her mother, who gave a snort from her nostrils.

'There will be no call for such a thing,' said Lady Blackwell, raising her chin to give me a watery glare.

Then she turned her head in a deliberate fashion, not to disturb her mass of powdered hair, and looked at the clock on the mantlepiece. 'We should say our goodbyes, Elizabeth,' she said to her daughter.

'Nonsense, mother. We have only just arrived. Do go on, Mr Hall.' She turned her smile towards me, displaying all her fine teeth. 'I am most curious to know about the nature of your protection.'

I attempted a light laugh and brushed a speck of dust from my breeches, feeling very inconvenienced by the surplus heat that was entering the room through my earlobes.

'What I meant to say,' I said, turning from one lady to the next, adopting that solemn, nodding motion once employed by my late father, when he interviewed clients in this very parlour, 'what I mean is that you shall have my utmost vigilance in this matter. My teas are procured from traders of impeccable reputation. I test all their consignments personally. You shall find no terra-japonica, log-wood or liquorice in my leaf, nor any other impurity.'

'Well then,' said Miss Blackwell, pouring her bright gaze into the centre of my face. 'We shall have the protection of your nose. I feel safer already.'

The volume of blood circulating in my ears had become distracting, so my memory of the next few minutes is not perfect. But I believe things went awry in the following fashion:

'Tea!' said Lady Blackwell, rattling her cup in its saucer. 'We shall want more tea, and such, if we are to stay.'

But when I rang the bell, to summon the daily help, it had no effect, except to give me the air of an amateur campanologist. I rang it again; then again. At last, I took hold of the teapot with my own hands and spilt a great amount of its contents on the rug.

'Oh dear,' said Miss Blackwell. 'Shall I go into the kitchen to fetch the girl? I am sure she is dozing.'

She began to rise from her seat, which raised the pitch in her mother's throat to a screech.

'You shall see no such kitchen!' said the matron, levering herself from the couch. 'We shall find our carriage this minute, or some such that will take us. You sir,' she nodded at me, 'go into the street and find our man.' She drew her skirts together, in preparation for their exit.

Feeling somewhat aggrieved, I went to the shop and passed that errand to my apprentice, before returning to the parlour. Miss Blackwell took a step towards me and seemed likely to speak, but her mother broke in.

'We shall wait here, just the two of us,' said Lady Blackwell, in a cold tone. 'We will not keep you from your business any further.'

I burned visibly as I quit the apartment – there was no hiding it – but moments later I heard sharp words between mother and daughter, then the young lady's step as she entered the shop behind me. This was followed by a piteous sound from the parlour: Lady Blackwell called her daughter's name in a wailing cry, more like a swan's bray than a human voice.

Shaking, I busied myself at the counter, measuring out two ounces of Souchong, which Lady Blackwell had chosen earlier, for the benefit of her health, when our interview had still been cordial. I did not look up at the young lady as she approached, but split much of the tea on the marble counter. She waited a moment before speaking, watching me scoop the precious leaves back into the bag. They she spread her forearms on the counter, so that the dove grey of her gloves lay inches from my hands.

'I am most disappointed,' she said, in a bright tone, with just the smallest catch of her breath behind it. 'I feel certain that we could have brewed a delightful pot in the kitchen, and not needed your girl at all.'

I was lumpen and had no remarkable answer. 'I am

sure a lady of your station should not make tea,' I said, at last. 'Especially with a shopkeeper.'

She put her glove on my hand and I jerked as if burned.

'Ah, but the world is changing,' she said. 'Did you not know? They have declared for independence in America, and all because of a spillage of tea. What do you think of that, Mr Hall?'

She bent her head low towards me as she spoke, but I kept my eyes on my work. I felt the brown light of the shop on my shoulders, smelt the perfume of all the bales and sacks around me, their treasure of tea leaves and coffee beans, blue figs and ginger. I burned with yearning as I occupied myself with tying the packet, but my courage failed me.

'I am sure I do not know,' I told her, holding the wrapped Souchong in my hand, feeling the comfort of its everyday warmth.

My apprentice came through the door, chiming the bell and flushing chilled air and brightness into the room. He gaped at us.

'You must excuse me,' I said, looking past the girl's pale face. 'I must take this to your mother.'

UGLY AS SIN *and other clichés*

All's Fair in Love and War

Sue Wright

The dead soldier lay face down in the mud while the rain rattled the helmet beside him. The letter in his pocket was folded inside a tobacco tin where it would remain, unread by the girl back home. When the boot of an enemy soldier nudged the head of the dead man and turned it, there was no longer a recognisable face. Greedy fingers reached under the body, curled around the medal and tugged hard to rip it away from the fabric, making the legs move. The change in position eased the tin out of the pocket and as the thief made away, the swivel of his heel pushed it deeper into the mud.

By the time winter turned to spring, the rotting flesh had begun to ooze and as the water laden fibres of the dead man's jacket began to warm, millions of microbes started work on reintegrating the whole sodden mess into the soil.

The girl back home danced with other soldiers although none of them wore medals.

When the killing stopped, the terrain returned to stillness. Only the breath of exertion accompanied the boots that now criss-crossed the mud. A hundred hands pulled out the broken body parts and a hundred more piled high the tools of war. For years, they shifted tons of barbed wire, shrapnel, bullets and bombs but they could not clear it all. Piece by piece, nature clawed back what had always been hers. Even so, the iron harvest continued long after the fields had been returned to farming.

One late summer evening just as the sun touched the horizon, a farmer put two fingers between his lips and let out an ear splitting whistle. His dog looked up briefly, but continued to scrabble at the edge of a furrow until he released a small rusty tobacco tin. The farmer's gnarled hand reached down and picked it up; he prised off the lid with a grimy thumb and took out the folded paper inside. His work-worn hands were ill equipped to tease the paper apart. He finished what time and the elements had begun and he and the dog watched the fragments fall.

Nothing was left of what the soldier had felt about the girl back home.

All Fur Coat and No Knickers

Dawn Wyndham

The band was setting up on the steps of the broad carved stone entrance to the church.

'Testing, testing. One-two. On-er, a-two-er. Sibilance. Sssibilance'

Harry un-hooked his guitar strap from his shoulder, smiling across at his newly-announced fiancée, Christelle. He had moved to France five years earlier. Unsure of his commitment to almost everything, he held on to his Croydon semi and rented it out, using the rent to fund the mortgage on the Maison de Maître that was now his home and his business. Wearing a pink vest and frayed shorts he had acquired a Gallic charm. He smelled of stale Gauloises, his teeth surprisingly white against his face, brown as a chestnut. He had a joint behind his ear and his hair in a loose ponytail running down his back. He was wearing dusty sliders that meant he had this lanky, shuffling walk. Nothing was ever a hurry with Harry.

As the afternoon sun lost its heat and dipped its head, the party was just getting started. In front of the huge gothic church in Le Dorat the village square was filling up with people. Laughing, greeting each other noisily, the clatter of plates and cutlery, wineglasses and bottles being laid down on the long trestle tables to keep space, friends guarding places for those who were yet to arrive amidst children running, giggling and excited.

'Salut!'

'Bon soirée'

'Alain, T'as été où mon pote?'

'Pierre! Viens ici!'

It was the final Farmers' Market of the summer, a Marché Nocturne; everyone congregated not to shop, but to eat and make merry. The market traders were mostly old men in flat caps with dusty aprons, money belts around their waists. The butcher's stall set out with meats and sausages, wetly glistening blood red and white amidst the vivid parsley. Leafy salads on the next stall clothed in ripe shades of green, yellow, ochre and scarlet. The wine stall where you could get your own bottle filled from oak barrels. The bread stall, the cheese stall, the one that sold the delicious patisserie and last, but not least, the frites stall cooking fresh crispy French fries that would soon have the throng of a queue in front of it. Each stall covered by its own blue and white striped canopy or different coloured umbrella. Smells to make you drool. A long bank of flat charcoal-filled racks to cook on was ranged alongside the church wall, wafting wood-scented smoke across the sea of tables in the square.

On a far corner, just in front of the Tabac, a group of British expats were raising the first toast of the night. The roar of a Harley Davidson shattered the conversation briefly as it drew to a halt close to where they sat.

'Bon soirée,' she sang as she dismounted, unfolding her leather-clad long legs and pulling herself up to her full six foot height. Sylvie messed up her peroxide hair with her fingers, arranged an outrageous fake fox fur over her bare shoulders and plonked her open-face helmet on the table.

''Ow are you?' she asked as she stooped to air-kiss both cheeks of Bob's face.

'Ze building work ees going well, Non?'

Every one of the Brits seemed to have an ongoing renovation project, adding the French for beams, plumbing and drains to their vocabulary. He laughed.

'Yes, it's going fine, we should be ready for you to plaster the walls next week.' His head was level with her breasts, displayed to fine advantage by her tight, low-cut white t-shirt. Muscling her way into a space to sit she smiled at the assembly, singling out the men for extra eye contact.

'So, tonight we 'ave fun, n'est-ce-pas?'

Kay, Bob's wife whispered to Jessica, next to her.

'There she goes again.' Jessica kicked her ankle under the table.

Across the square Harry looked up as he heard the bike's noise above the crowd. He pursed his lips and sighed, pretending intense concentration on tuning his guitar.

'Damn her', he thought.

He pulled out his Zippo, lit his joint and blew out a plume of smoke.

Three months earlier it had been so different.

'No!'

His fist had slammed down on the table.

'Enough!'

She turned, her face a mess of mascara, tears streaming. They were the same height, eye to eye, the pain and anger evident on both their faces. They had been rowing for hours.

'But, 'Arry, zis ees our business. We built it togezzer. We can't split up. I can't leave. Zees is an 'otel for bikers, like you and me, not like 'er.' She spat the last word with venom. It was true. Route du Sud, a hotel converted three years before from a large 'maison de maître' on the main avenue had become a successful bikers' stop-over on the route south to Spain. It had been Harry's money, but it was Sylvie's flair and local contacts that had made the difference.

She had suspected something, but not this complete confession, this stark admission of his infidelity. It was a reckless blade that sliced them apart.

'C'mon Sylvie, let's get something for the fire,' said Jessica, linking her arm into Sylvie's and giving it a squeeze.

Shoulder to shoulder they wandered across to the meat stall, an incongruous pair of friends. Jessica, a dumpy English rose, considerably shorter and, at forty-five, ten years older. She wore a denim skirt and vest with thick strappy sandals, her shaggy auburn hair loose around her shoulders. Sylvie walked with a blatant hip-sway that said 'Sensuality'. She enjoyed the male attention she attracted, knowing that many eyes followed her. She wondered if his eyes were following her too.

'So, how're you doing?' asked Jessica. A bug landed on her arm and she flicked it off.

'Oh, zere ees lots of work and my new 'ouse ees OK.'

'That's not what I meant. How are you doing, really?'

Sylvie stopped walking.

'Jess, I...' she faltered. 'Oh, Jess!' A stifled sob. A look of panic flashed across her face. 'Can we go to somewhere ees more quiet?'

In the ladies toilets at the back of the bar Jessica and Sylvie huddled in a cubicle. Through tears and whispers it all poured out.

'How many weeks? Jessica asked with shocked concern.

'L'hôpital, they say about thirteen weeks!' Sylvie was crying now.

Jessica blew a sort of whistle through her teeth.

'You must have known before now, surely?'

'Non, I sought eet was ze upset of ze break-up.'

'You're sure it's Harry's? I mean you look as if you've been, er, putting it about a bit lately...'

Sylvie shook her head, an ironic laugh on her lips.

'Eet is all a façade, Jess. To show 'im – and 'er – zat I don't care. Really I 'ave been dying.' Jessica held her as she wept, this big woman in biker's leathers a child in her arms.

'What will you do?' Sylvie's French Catholic upbringing made abortion impossible.

'I do not know,' Sylvie sighed. 'I really do not know. For now I will say I 'ave a 'eadache and go 'ome.'

'Want me to come with you?'

'Non, ees Ok.'

'Well, we can't stay here all night.' She moved. 'I've got cramp.' They both smiled, the tension broken. 'C'mon.'

Jessica stood and unlocked the door. As they stepped out of the cubicle they were greeted by Christelle, stock still, a horrified look on her face. They were all frozen for a full second before she fled.

As Sylvie climbed the stairs there was a knock on the door. Tightening the belt on her dressing gown, she set her cup on a step and pulled back the latch.

'Sylvie, we need to talk…' said Harry.

Panic Button

Kathy Miles

'Mad old cow,' Lydia said as she spooned a teaspoon of sugar into her latte. The three of them were sitting in Café Nero, watching the elderly woman in the corner. The woman was alone – her fierce, upright position making it clear that she didn't welcome company – and was slowly and deliberately squashing a fly that had the misfortune to land on the plateful of cake crumbs in front of her. It wasn't the action itself that had attracted the girls' attention, but the evident enjoyment that the woman was taking in it. Lydia shuddered.

'Probably lives by herself with a couple of dozen cats, and a dead husband in the basement,' Jenny said.

'Bet she killed him,' Amy grinned. 'A baseball bat, maybe, or a swift blow to the head with an antique bronze statue.'

'Nah. She'll have done him in with a cup of poisoned tea. My dad watches all these Agatha Christie murders, it's always poison.'

Jenny reached for her phone and Googled 'Ways to Kill Your Husband.'

'Hey, there's actually a book on it from Amazon!

How to Murder Your Husband. Imagine!'

They giggled.

'Better not let your mum see it, Lydia, or your dad'll be the next one.'

The woman looked across; she must have guessed they were talking about her. Even from several tables away Lydia could see how very dark her eyes were. The woman met Lydia's gaze, and Lydia felt a sudden desperate need to get out of the café.

'Hey, let's go, ' she said.

'I've still got half a cup of coffee.'

Lydia stood up.

'Well, I want to go shopping. Catch me up in the precinct.'

The café was much too hot. Her breath was coming fast, as if there were bats beating inside her chest. She could feel the vein in her neck, blood pushing against the skin. She stumbled to the door, wanting fresh air, the sound of traffic in her ears, the reassuring sight of the street. The woman smiled at her as she passed. It was a strange, tight-lipped smile that didn't show her teeth. Lydia instinctively put out a hand as if to ward it off. And then she was outside, and there were cars bleeping, a siren in the distance, a bus passing by, and things were normal, just a usual Saturday shopping trip with the girls. She breathed slowly and carefully until the panic passed. She was used to these attacks. They could strike at any time, anywhere. She just had to wait until this one was over. She took the diazepam from her bag, wondered if this time she needed to take one, and thought that perhaps she'd walk to the precinct first and sit down for a while.

Back in Café Nero, Jenny and Amy were eyeing up the woman, who had finished killing the fly, and was idly stirring her tea. Jenny noticed that she hadn't actually drunk any of it.

'Bit weird to get a cup of tea and not drink it,' she said.

Amy shrugged.

'Maybe the fly went into the tea before landing on the plate. Or maybe she's lonely, and the tea's just an excuse to avoid going home.'

'Well, you'd not want to go home with a dead husband in the basement, would you?' Jenny said.

'Or maybe she's homeless?'

But the woman didn't look homeless. She was dressed in an odd assortment of clothes; a long black skirt, red and orange striped sweater, layers of t-shirts peeking out from underneath, and a pair of expensive-looking boots. Her bag looked expensive, too, a large leather shoulder bag with a brand-label, and a chiffon scarf tied to the handle. A black woollen coat was slung over the back of her chair.

'That's a Hermes scarf,' Jenny said. 'My mum's got a similar one. Bet she's loaded. Good job all her life, teaching or something, and a whacking great pension to live on.'

'Plus the inheritance from the dead husband,' Amy

added. 'That's probably why she did him in.'

The woman got up, put on her coat, and moved towards the door. She walked awkwardly, stumbling slightly. As she reached the door, she took out a pair of dark sunglasses and slipped them on, as though the thin winter sunshine was much too harsh.

'Shall we go and find Lydia?'

'Yes, OK.'

In the precinct, Lydia was feeling calmer. She hadn't taken a pill. She was trying not to, to keep them for when the anxiety was so great that she was unable to move, turned into a stone statue where the world raced around her and she was separated from it by a huge armour-plated window. She was being silly. The woman was just an old lady who was annoyed at being laughed at. There was nothing sinister about her. She had killed a fly, that's all, and Lydia had had a panic attack. She checked her phone, and saw that the girls were over in River Island and wanted her to join them. She got up from the bench she'd been sitting on and began to walk down the main part of the precinct. It was busy today. Christmas just over, the sales on, and the whole town had piled into the shopping area eager for bargains. A dress in a window caught her attention. Down from £70 to £15. She stood there wondering if she had time to try it on before meeting up with Jenny and Amy again. Probably not. And she didn't really need a new dress.

As she turned away, she saw her. The woman was standing about ten yards away, and was staring intently at Lydia. Lydia started to shake. Yet this was ridiculous, for surely the woman was only looking at the window display? 'Get a grip,' she told herself. And then the woman was standing in front of her, she had her hand on Lydia's shoulder, and Lydia was gasping for breath and the world was spinning, and her neck, why was her neck hurting so much, and where had all the blood come from, why hadn't anyone noticed that Lydia was bleeding, and why was the woman smiling, what was happening, why was there blood on the woman's mouth, and where, where, where had everyone gone?

UGLY AS SIN *and other clichés*

Another Nail in the Coffin

Sue Wright

Naked, apart from a pair of black tights, fine as silk with a sheen that emphasised the curve of her calf, Melissa sat on a velvet stool surrounded by discarded clothing. She stretched a leg forward with pointed toe and ran her hands from ankle to thigh to ensure that there were no twists or wrinkles. Bending her knee so the leg aligned neatly with the other, she reached across to the bed to pick up her favourite red silk bra, which she fastened before adjusting her breasts to their best advantage. The exquisite cut of her new black dress was designed to reveal more than a hint of cleavage.

With her hair pulled back beneath a temporary Alice band, she took a slow critical look at her face in the mirror. Her eyes were wide and dark above cheekbones perfectly set in a heart-shaped face. She proceeded to add a range of cosmetic products that guaranteed that her fifty years would not be revealed by the skin of her face. Her eyebrows and lashes were perfectly groomed and she chose a deep cardinal red lipstick.

She stood and reached for the dress, slipping it

over her slender shoulders and zipping it up carefully so as not to mark the perfectly painted nails. Her dark hair was cropped short and merely required a flick of her hands to remove the temporary restraint and allow the natural curl to regain its tousled chic. It was a look that was the envy of many women half her age. She chose simple gold hoop earrings and a bangle to match before sliding her feet into her newest Manolo Blahniks, the softest black leather with gold trim. She smoothed her skirt down and turned her leg, the better to admire the golden heel. A glance in the hall mirror ensured that the black velvet pillbox hat sat the way she wanted it and veiled her eyes. Her faux fur coat was warm and capacious and she clasped the wide collar together with its secret fastening just as the soft rap of gloved hands could be heard at the front door.

The chauffeur ushered her into the gleaming sedan where she sat alone with her thoughts while they drove through the city. Tower blocks gave way to high street shops and rows of B&Bs and small hotels and were superseded by domestic terraces. As the buildings became smaller, the density of people became greater. Melissa watched the crowds milling along like so many ants and then she became aware of the driver looking at her in his rear view mirror. When she caught his eye, he looked away and she smiled to herself.

When they reached the crematorium there was already a thickening stream of black clad humanity trailing its way towards the entrance. The crowd parted to let them through and closed in again behind. Even though her eyes were hidden behind the veil she looked straight ahead. Only the driver saw the expression on the faces of those who looked at her. His own face was inscrutable.

Inside the crematorium, the coffin was on a dais at the front and the dead man was exposed to view. He looked peaceful, pale and handsome. In death there was a youthfulness about him that belied his years. He wore a dark suit with a favourite tie, sky blue, the colour of his eyes, although they of course were not open to view. One by one the people filed past on the way to their seats. Some stared, some averted their eyes, and none were weeping. The man in the coffin, impassive in death revealed nothing of his erstwhile nature. The family was already seated, his wife and adult children arranged in order of seniority.

Melissa was the last to enter the room and the sound of her heels affirmed her presence. She had undone the fastening at the neck of her coat and let it hang open. A complex mixture of fear, envy and lust flowed towards her and she shivered a little. As she approached the coffin, she ran her hand across the surface of the roped hand rail and snagged a fingernail. The perfect red nail that had been glued on only that morning pulled loose and fell in, alongside the man whose wealth had paid for it.

She grimaced at the exposed natural nail over which she placed the pad of her thumb and took her seat in the front pew. Something in the eulogy caused a very slight upturn to one corner of her mouth. Perhaps it was mention of his devotion to his family, or maybe his fondness for fine wine. Indeed he had left behind a very comprehensive collection at the apartment. Not only wines but artworks too. Should she choose to sell any of them there would be considerable financial gain. To be sure, he had left her well provided for.

She glanced across at the wife, whose narrow lips were tightly pressed together. They were eye to eye for less than a second but it was the wife who looked away.

Weighed in the Balance

Dawn Morgan

At close to noon on the March equinox, Dai Morgan's life hung in the balance. He wasn't aware of the date as he clung to the branch above his head, almost chest deep in the fast-flowing river, his feet scrabbling against stones. He wasn't pondering the fact that the earth was poised between seasonal tilts, while he was hanging on the edge of life. He was too busy fighting with the river. But he was the kind of man who would have been pleased by this cosmic symmetry, if he'd been sitting in safety on the shore.

As noon passed and the earth tipped towards summer, Dai assessed his chances. He'd been calculating his danger since the moment he'd walked into the river's stronger current. He'd measured the force of the water against his thighs, felt the mass of the Cambrian Mountains that drove the river down the valley, and judged that he could stand against it, for a while. If he hadn't slipped, he would still be standing there in his waders, feeling a bite on his line.

After his tumble he had stayed calm, looked quickly ahead. He'd grabbed this long willow branch as he passed under it. Despite its slenderness, it held his weight. He would be ashore by now, except that the branch overhung a deeper part of the river and he couldn't get his footing. After only a minute, his hands had become numb and his waders had filled with water. He wriggled and used his toes to remove them and felt a moment of relief as they slithered away into the stream. But his plight was still severe. There were no other branches in the path he would take if he loosened his grip on this willow; just rocks that would open his skull. He swallowed down a spike of fear.

For the first time in twenty years of fishing, he almost wished he'd been more sociable. Further down the bank, other club members were opening their lunch packs in companionable huddles, releasing aromas of bread, tomato and coffee into the moss-scented air. To his surprise, Dai found himself on the verge of tears as he pictured the warmth of the scene. But he fought back the prickling sensation and took a breath, gripping more tightly to the branch.

More than most men, Dai was able to set emotions aside to deal with the facts. Closing his eyes against the dun-coloured landscape, he willed his thoughts into order.

Downriver, a fellow fisherman was shaking the last drops of coffee from a plastic cup.

'I wonder how Dai's getting on?' he mused.

'Probably bagged a ten-pounder,' said a companion.

'Do you think he'll need help landing that?' asked

another, closing his sandwich box.

'Ha!' said the first man. 'Not Dai.'

'Well, maybe he'll want some help eating it?'

'Ha ha!'

The first man shook his head and slipped his flask into a rucksack. The three companions went back to their fishing, adding their restful sounds to the peace of the riverbank.

Upstream, Dai felt his arms weaken as the river pressed against him, drawing his blood-heat into its flow. He judged that his best hope was to edge along the branch towards the bank, which was about three metres away. If he could move even slightly towards it, he might find purchase for his feet. Pulling upwards with his right arm to take the weight, he shifted his left hand along the branch with a lurch of strength, then grunted with pain and repeated the action with his other hand, gaining ten centimetres. He couldn't afford to rest. Baring his teeth with the effort he completed the sequence again, and again. Then horror surged through him: the water deepened towards the bank. He strained against the riverbed with the tips of his boots and felt hope slide away.

In the next valley, Dai's wife was preparing Sunday dinner. They ate their roast in the evening during the fishing season, but in all other ways they observed the weekly ritual of roast beef, coffee and the Sunday papers. Everything in order. It had been that way throughout their marriage, even when the boys were at home. Kate glanced through the kitchen window and imagined Dai by the river, enjoying his solitude.

'I wish you'd take the dog,' she'd told him that morning.

'No dogs allowed,' he replied.

'I know, but he'd be company.'

This conversation was also part of their Sunday routine. Years before, she would have pressed him to take the boys.

'They won't want to come,' he would say.

After a few years of Kate asking this question, the answer became true.

Before Dai left the house each Sunday, Kate would slide an extra biscuit into his pocket, like a talisman. He'd always make sure that he ate it, leaving the wrapper in his pocket for her to find.

In the final moment before Dai lost his grip, he uttered a cry. He'd never filled a sound with such passion, emptying his heart into a single yell. The noise carried downstream, causing several fishermen to turn their heads. Two men ran towards the sound, pushing through the undergrowth. They didn't see Dai in mid-stream, colliding with rocks and debris as he was swept away.

As he swirled in the water, Dai flinched at the grey shapes of the rocks. He winced, too, at his own raw thoughts, which rose ahead of him: his young sons' faces, looking out through the window as he strode to the car each Sunday morning and packed his fishing bag; the eyes of his dog as he left her behind, forgiving him even as he left her; the wrapped biscuit from Kate, still uneaten in his pocket. At this final thought, he heard his voice add a wail to the water's rumble and he tried to clutch his arms to his chest; but the flow was too strong. Embraced by the river, he passed to the sea, collecting bruises that would never blossom.

UGLY AS SIN *and other clichés*

A Blot on the Landscape

Sal Starling

Something wasn't quite right.

He studied the painting once more.

The autumn sunset with its looming dark clouds on the horizon was pretty good - his best painting to date, he thought. He admired the trees flanking each side of the canvas, satisfied they were more realistic and treelike than the lollipop shapes he'd tended to paint before taking art lessons. His paintwork was also becoming more impasto, he noted, giving greater texture and movement to his landscape. The sheep needed a little more work, but he was generally pleased with his effort - apart from one niggling little thing; the cottage. It wasn't quite right.

I'll sleep on it, he thought.

Dennis cleaned his hands, hung up his apron and deadheaded a few sweet-peas on the way from his painting shed to the kitchen door; he wiped his feet and pulled off his shoes.

'Don't forget to put your shoes on the newspaper and wash your hands, dear.'

Dennis knew this was coming. Betty said the same thing every time he came in from the garden or the shed. As always, he did as she asked.

Immediately after dinner, Betty washed, dried and put away the dishes. Dennis used to offer, but Betty said that he didn't do it right. She liked the china to be placed in size order; the cup handles all to face the same way and the cutlery to sit meticulously straight in the drawer.

It hadn't always been like this. When they first married, their life was much the same as others in the street. They lived happily with unmade beds, cupboards full of chipped crockery, and cushions squashed into the corners of an old sofa. Hoovering was done occasionally, polishing rarely.

Dennis's painting shed still reflected those days. It was his bolt-hole, his secluded place of freedom where untidiness, clutter and disorder reigned supreme. Organised chaos, that's what he liked. Jars full of brushes and squashed tubes of paint sat on roughly hewn shelves, and assorted oily rags hung from nails in the framework. The floor was an abstract of dried paint - flicked or dropped from his brush. Half painted canvases hung lop-sided from rusty nails, or lay in random spaces around the shed, and a pile of wrappers from chocolate biscuits he sneaked in from the corner shop overflowed from a cardboard box in the corner. Dennis loved his shed; Betty didn't. She said it was too untidy and smelled of turps and never ventured inside.

Dennis also loved to paint and, since attending evening classes, had learned much about colour, perspective and tone which he began to use with increasing confidence in his paintings. Painting was something he had all to himself, unhindered, unconstrained.

That evening they sat in the living room with a cup of tea, two digestives and Coronation Street. Dennis would like to have put his feet up on the coffee table and dunked biscuits into his tea, but that would be untidy and would upset Betty.

Betty's compulsive behaviour had begun to invade their lives after her third miscarriage many years ago. The doctor explained it was probably a reaction to the trauma - shock can do strange things to people he'd said - but Betty believed she lost her babies because she had picked up a bug, or had dirty hands, or didn't keep her home clean enough. Over the years, Dennis lost his wife to her obsession.

The next morning, Dennis filled his flask and headed off to the shed, leaving Betty cleaning windows for the fourth time that week. Sitting on a stool, he surveyed his autumn landscape. What *was* it about the cottage that didn't look right? He put the painting aside and set up another canvas. With a wash of burnt umber he sketched out a street scene lined with lamp posts. A practice in perspective.

After dinner, Dennis kissed his wife and left her to her daily bathroom-cleaning ritual while he went to his art class.

That evening he learned about the 'golden ratio'.

He discovered the mathematics in art and how this magical ratio of aesthetics was used by the great artists to produce wonderful works of art with symmetry, balance and beauty. He saw how DaVinci used it in his paintings of 'The Last Supper' and the 'Mona Lisa', and how Michaelangelo's 'Creation of Adam' has God and Adam's fingertips meeting at precisely the golden ratio point. Although the mathematical formula was difficult to grasp, Dennis could see it at work in the art of the old masters. It is that precise point where something just looks *right*.

On the way home, Dennis thought about the clock on their mantelpiece; he often wondered why Betty always placed it exactly where she did - not quite in the centre, but not quite at the end. If it were down to Dennis he would have the clock in the middle, probably with a matching candlestick at each end for balance. Sometimes he would move the clock a touch to one side, but later in the day he would find it returned to its original place. It was his secret game. One day he even measured its distance from the edge of the shelf. She always replaced it in exactly the same spot and, he had to admit, it looked right. Betty instinctively knew the aesthetic beauty of the golden ratio.

Later that evening, Betty asked about his art lesson, listened without understanding, and kissed him goodnight. Her evening had been busier than usual, but she would still take her sleeping pill after three times checking the windows and doors were secure, and that her bedroom curtains were closed evenly without a gap.

The following morning, Dennis headed off to the shed. The first thing he noticed was the smell of bleach. Heart sinking, he looked around his sanctuary.

The table was scrubbed clean of the old, dried blobs of paint and a neat row of perfectly cleaned brushes lay across it in size order, old jam jars had been replaced with pristine, neatly labelled tubs; the rags had gone, replaced by a kitchen roll dispenser, and tubes of paint - their caps replaced - lay across the shelf in a rainbow order of reds, yellows, greens and blues. On the floor sprawled a new rose-pink rug covered with a sheet of clear plastic. His canvases had been neatly stacked against the wall in size order, except for one; on the easel stood his autumn landscape. He moved closer, wondering what it was that was different. He took a long, slow breath. The cottage, once at the centre of the canvas, had been carefully scraped off and its outline neatly redrawn a little higher and to the right. It looked perfect.

When Betty found Dennis his feet were suspended just a few centimetres off the floor. His hanging would have been unsuccessful had the shed roof been a little lower.

Two years to the day, Betty left the cemetery after placing a rainbow of silk flowers on Dennis's grave and blowing him a kiss.

On returning home, she kicked off her shoes in

the hallway, draped her coat on the bannister and made a cup of tea. She flicked a steaming teabag into the sink full of dishes, took a few biscuits from the tin, sat on the sofa and placed her feet on the coffee table, one foot sliding a pile of magazines and chocolate wrappers to the floor. She glanced towards the mantelpiece.

'That clock needs moving,' she said to herself, dunking a hobnob into her tea.

At the Drop of a Hat

Sue Wright

It was an old fashioned shop with an old fashioned bay window with small square panes of glass. In order to see the goods on display you had to stand really close or go inside. Nevertheless, the newest creations were always on show. There was only space for three or four, depending on the size of the hats. Mr George leaned back a little, the better to see the tempting effect of his new arrangement.

He was a tall man with black hair that belied his years and a splendid moustache to match. His pin-striped suit showed his languid stance to advantage, and a silk handkerchief frothed from his top pocket, just the right shade of magenta to offset the shirt and tie. His cufflinks were platinum and worth a considerable amount of money, but his shoes, though shined to perfection, were not as new as he would have liked.

A discordant jangle accompanied the door opening. This evoked a grimace from Mr George, but he rapidly composed himself and offered the lady his most beatific smile, revealing the whitest most even teeth that his dentist had been able to provide.

The little woman who stood hesitantly in the doorway was hatless, which prompted a particular gleam in Mr George's eyes as he walked towards her and ushered her inside the shop, closing the door firmly behind her. He swivelled smartly on one heel and led her to a velvet chair at the far end of the shop facing a large gilded mirror.

She perched on the edge of the seat and frowned at her reflected image while Mr George adjusted the lighting and tutted around her head and neck. He folded his arms and placed a finger to one side of his mouth as he contemplated her gingery blonde curls that hadn't seen a hairdresser's scissors in far too long. She ran her fingers through her hair in a nervous gesture and turned her pale blue gaze towards him.

Mr George let out an inadvertent squeal and rushed to the window, returning to her side proffering a wild and riotous concoction in organza and lace, festooned with feathers and beads.

She nodded her assent and he placed the azure pillbox to one side of her head and hid the elastic that would hold it, among the profusion of curls. He then adjusted the veil, revealing a narrow band of fine embroidery from which dropped several strands of tiny pearls. Her shiver of delight set them aglow. The peacock feathers that coiled to the side were shown in their full glory when Mr George held up his favourite ebony hand mirror so that she could see the back.

A flush came to her cheeks to brighten her face, and the blue of the silk brought out the colour of her eyes. Mr George stood back to admire his handiwork.

'Ravishing, don't you think?'

His hearing was perfectly good but her whispered reply appeared to have vanished amongst the feathers.

Unaware that she had spoken, Mr George reached for a large blue and gold striped hat box which he proceeded to fill with tissue. He carefully removed the hat from her head and lovingly placed it inside, where it nestled discreetly in the paper.

She tried again.

'How much is it please?'

On hearing his reply, she blanched and rolled her eyes. He watched in horror as she toppled backwards, clutching the handle of the hatbox. In a flurry of skirts, tissue paper, feathers and cardboard she fell into the luxurious pile of the tasteful grey carpet.

Mr George rushed to her side, his moustache quivering. He carefully retrieved this most glorious confection of the milliner's craft. Evidently, his consummate skill with tissue paper had prevented any damage, and with his blood pressure rapidly returning to normal, he restored it to its rightful place in the window. A lugubrious clang from the doorbell at his back told him that the lady had left the shop.

UGLY AS SIN *and other clichés*

That's Life

Dawn Wyndham

Birth.

School.

Work.

Taxes.

Death.

Printed in Great Britain
by Amazon